KISS THE KREMLIN GOODBYE

Other books by Alison Leonard

The Crest of the Dragon
Gate-crashing the Dream Party
An Inch of Candle
Tinker's Career
You and the Quakers
You've Got It Wrong Again, Gabriel (play)

KISS THE KREMLIN GOODBYE

ALISON LEONARD

WALKER BOOKS
LONDON

First published 1991 by Walker Books Ltd
87 Vauxhall Walk, London SE11 5HJ

© 1991 Alison Leonard

First printed 1991
Printed in Great Britain by
Billings and Son, Worcester

British Library Cataloguing in Publication Data
Leonard, Alison
Kiss the kremlin goodbye.
I. Title
823'.914[F]

ISBN 0-7445-2134-3

I'd like to thank Mr Clive Thompson and
his colleagues at the British Embassy in Moscow
and assure him that they bear no resemblance to
the characters in Chapter 11. Many thanks, too,
to Irini, Tatiana, Yevgeny and the two Annas, Larissa,
Tanya, Nadya and her daughter, Lara and Rachel and
the Quaker Youth Theatre, Vanya and Alexander
and the Moscow University Students' Theatre
(no resemblance here either), Howard, and Dorothy.
And to teachers and pupils of the Simon Langton
Schools, Canterbury, of Leighton Park, Reading,
and of Maes Garmon, Mold. And, as always,
Frank and the girls.

*"Oh why may I not love them both at once?" she
kept asking herself in the depths of bewilderment…
"One thing is certain," she thought, "to tell Prince
Andrei what has happened, or to hide it from him,
is equally impossible."*

Tolstoy, War and Peace

There was a moment when it seemed she didn't
have to choose. They stood, she and Kostya, about
ten cobbles apart in the vastness of Red Square,
and instead of taking two steps forward, he leaned
over the airy space between them and gave her lips
the lightest kiss. Her kiss was feather-light in
return. It asked no questions, demanded no
commitment. Dafydd seemed to be there with her.
He was in her bloodstream. Home was there as
well – the gate swinging between stone walls, the
narrow lane down the wooded hill to the village.
It was all contained within her as she leaned
forward to kiss Kostya in Red Square.

In some other world, where questions need
never be asked and choices need never be made,
perhaps Kostya, the kiss in Red Square, the blurred
swaying of the Metro, his gift of the tiny icon in
her hand – they could all have come to Clwyd and
been contained. But in this world, it could not
be so.

CHAPTER ONE

I dream of Moscow every night.

Chekhov, *Three Sisters*

Megan passionately wanted to go to Moscow. "I *need* to go," she said. She couldn't imagine the party taking off from Heathrow without her.

But Ellen – "Miss Tudor-Williams" as they had to call her in Bryn Corach and Pentre High Schools – was impervious to pleading. Every Tuesday and Thursday in drama lessons Megan had pleaded, and every Friday evening at Drama Club. But neither Megan's hysteria nor anyone else's mute begging would budge Ellen. How would she choose? No one knew. Even those who'd played the lead in this year's productions weren't guaranteed.

In the end, she chose equal numbers of English and Welsh. "Political," some said, "to be so fair about it." And equal numbers of each sex, too.

She made her announcement on the first Friday evening of the autumn term. The clatter faded to silence, but she waited still one more moment. Megan felt her contact lenses itching in her eyes, a sure sign of strain.

"Meredydd Edwards," Ellen began, her voice so low that they all had to lean forward. "Olwen Evans. Abigail Haigh." Abi was in, so Megan must surely be. Megan had played Anita in *West Side Story*, though it took hours making her skin look Puerto Rican, and Abi had to put up with being her understudy.

"James Haydock..." Gentleman Jim? A murmur went round, easing the tension. Jim smiled in embarrassment. "Llyr Hughes-Jones – Mari and Tom Lewis – "

Not Dafydd Morgan, because Dafydd didn't come to drama. Anyway, there was nothing between Megan and Dafydd any more.

"Annest Rhys..." Shipway should come next. "Michelle Skillicorn."

So Megan hadn't been chosen – Dad was right – she wasn't "mature" enough! Mature – Dad's favourite word. Well, she was younger than Kate – how was she expected to be mature, when Kate got all the attention because of her wretched asthma...? She opened her mouth to scream, but nothing came out.

"Megan Shipway, Keith Speakman, and Richard Tighe. I think that's twelve."

Megan squeaked, "Ellen!"

"Yes, Megan?"

"Shipway comes before Skillicorn. In the alphabet."

"So it does. I'm sorry." Ellen smiled briefly and combed her fingers through her fine short hair.

Murmurs went up – *why not me? why him, her?* – but Megan hardly heard them. She was

10

going to Moscow. Ellen considered her mature even if Dad didn't.

"Thank you," said Ellen, quelling complaints with a single sweeping glance. "Those who aren't included will have an opportunity next time round. The adults are myself and Mr and Mrs Garth Jones." Mrs Garth Jones had retired from teaching last year, and everyone liked her. "The head will send letters to your parents giving travel arrangements." She folded her sheet of paper and walked over to her corner. Those who'd been left out wandered off dejectedly, and the twelve chosen ones did a war-dance in the middle of the studio floor.

Megan was still gleefully throwing herself about when she and Abi came out to wait for Mum's car. "Of course," she said, swinging round a goalpost in the middle of the tarmac, "there was no chance she wouldn't include a talent like mine."

Abi kicked her as she came round. "Talent? Sorry, did I miss something? It's just your hair. They'll have to lock you up once we get there – it'll drive Boris and Leonid wild."

Megan fluffed up her rust-coloured mane, half irritated, half hoping Abi was right. "We're not going to Moscow for *romance*, for God's sake. Gorby's Moscow – it's where everything's at, isn't it? Political zizz – dissidents jumping about in Red Square – theatre bursting out all over the place – and we'll be there to experience it all..."

Ellen had been on holiday to the Soviet Union, and met up with a friend of a friend called Oleg

11

Baranov. They found they were in the same job, teaching English and Drama, so what could be more obvious than getting their pupils together for an exchange? The date was fixed for the Pentre Corach Drama Club to go to Moscow the following November.

As soon as it was suggested, Megan set her heart on being one of the party. Ellen flew over in March to do the reconnoitre, and came back with photos of massive ice chunks floating down the Moskva River. After Easter she gave drama classes a Russian flavour, and introduced the Drama Club to chunks of Turgenev and Chekhov.

Oleg's original plan was for them to stay in a hostel. Ellen said, "Why not in each others' homes?" "Unheard of," he replied. "This is the Soviet Union, you realize. There are regulations: it must be a hostel. The hostel will not be gracious – please bring your own bath plugs and toilet paper. And tape measures to compete who can catch the longest cockroach." Cockroaches! Abi threw a mock faint at the prospect.

Then the turn-around came. "*Glasnost* has arrived with the school exchange," wrote Oleg. "Home-stay is possible!" So – they'd be staying in genuine Russian homes.

Summer arrived with a May heatwave. "Just when we've got to stay in and revise for GCSEs!" wailed the older ones, if they snatched time to get to Drama Club. Everyone wore T-shirts and jeans, all faces and arms and bare feet were brown. Only Megan had to ward off the sun because of her fair freckled skin. Then the holidays.

Megan always found summer the calmest time of the year at home. There were no midnight crises with Kate rushed off to hospital; not so much anxiety for Mum, so she calmed down and got on with her watercolours; Dad was on holiday and played endless cricket and tennis. This year they dared to stay in polluted old London with the grandparents on their way to Brittany, and after a fortnight's camping in all-day sunshine, four Shipways came back relaxed and fit. Mum even brought some of her paintings home with her instead of chucking them in a bin at St Malo harbour.

At the beginning of September it was school again, and Ellen's announcement of the Moscow twelve. The two schools, Welsh-speaking Bryn Corach and English-speaking Pentre, sat on a joint campus. Staff shortage had forced them to have drama lessons together – which meant "in English". The Welsh speakers were furious. No more drama classes in Welsh, no more productions like *Carousel*. They'd sung "When You Walk Through a Storm" like the climax of an Eisteddfod. The English-speakers weren't too thrilled either at having half the Puerto Ricans in their *West Side Story* sounding like football supporters from Cardiff Arms Park.

Now the Moscow trip caused more tension. Megan and the others couldn't mention it without getting catcalls – "Red Devils! Gorby's Gang!" Abi especially was a bundle of nerves. She was nipping out behind the toilet blocks more and more often for an illicit cigarette.

Megan had been friends with Abi Haigh ever since Abi had moved in next door. Abi was an only child. Her mother had a face beige with powder, and she parted her steely hair into three sharp triangles pulled into a bun at the back. She must have been born old, and seemed to think it was immoral to be young. Mr Haigh was abnormally tall and thin, with wisps of hair floating over his shiny baldness, and he didn't have any personality at all.

The nearer the day of departure, the worse Abi got. "Imagine! Them sniffing behind me for the tell-tale smell of fags – escaping with Boris or Leonid, and my aged parents with their binoculars out!" For her parents had insisted on joining the party.

At the parents' meeting, Ellen mentioned that each teenager would be staying in a Russian teenager's home.

"Tiny flats-a!" declared Mrs Haigh. Abi's mum always spat out an extra syllable when disgusted. "They don't even have proper bedrooms. They're forced to sleep on sofas-a!"

Then it emerged that Ellen would be home-staying too, in the flat of the teacher, Oleg Baranov, male. "He's an old friend of my family," Ellen told Mrs Haigh icily.

Mrs Haigh's skin was ice-resistant. "He's Russian. And a man-a. I think my husband and I had better join you on this trip, Miss Williams."

"*Tudor*-Williams."

"Book us a hotel room, will you? We'll pay whatever it takes-a. And one for Mr and Mrs Garth

Jones, and for yourself, Miss Williams. I insist."

So, thought Megan, Ellen has lost the chance of privacy with her Russian. How much does she care? From the tightly pursed lips, it was impossible to tell.

Abi hung round Megan. "I wish Ellen'd tell us what all this *glasnost* and *perestroika* stuff is about," she'd mutter into Megan's ear, and, "They say Gorbachev might be toppled any minute." Olwen Evans overheard her asking, "Where the hell's Estonia?" and chucked an atlas at her. Afterwards Megan furtively borrowed it, because she didn't know where Estonia was either.

Ellen turned Friday evenings into intensive Russian workshops. She invented exercises to help them understand "the Russian soul". "You're peasants on the Russian steppes. You've run out of cabbages and there's nothing to eat. You've got to go to the next village forty-five miles away, and you're famished, and it's bitter cold – twenty-five degrees below." This was the real stuff. Trying to get inside someone else's skin, ignoring the September sun outside and feeling as if there were frost hanging in your eyebrows.

Then she gave them a feel of tyranny, and of war. "By decree of our beloved Comrade Stalin," came the shrill command, "all farms belong to the Proletariat! Those failing to co-operate will be executed!" Megan tried to get herself shot, but always seemed to be out of the line of fire.

Worst of all was the Seige of Leningrad. "Close your eyes. Feel hungry. Starving. You've lived on a diet of two hundred and fifty calories a day for the last thirty months." Two hundred and fifty calories – less than one slice of chocolate gâteau! "Now. Move around like famine victims. You're searching for a dead dog to cook and eat."

Oh God, thought Megan, make me into someone like Ellen. Make me stop showing off, forget myself, forget to worry if my red sweatshirt goes with my purple trousers or whether I'd rather have pizza or spaghetti for tea. Let me get caught up in great events like the Berlin Wall or revolution in Moscow.

But it was exhausting. She'd look at the way Olwen Evans and Michelle Skillicorn, two of the sixth formers, were throwing themselves into it. Mish was small and square and energy-packed, and Olwen knew everything about theatre because her parents worked backstage. Olwen had real maturity, she didn't care what other people thought. She'd already been working with Russian tapes and was teaching Mish to say things like "Please could you tell me the way to the Finlandia Station?" Megan would have liked to offer them a lift home instead of Abi after Drama Club, but they both lived on the other side of the valley. Abi lived in the house that used to be Dafydd's.

During breaks, Megan would wonder whether to join Mish and Olwen discussing how a madman like Stalin could get into power. But then she'd decide against it and make for the corner where Spock and Tie were telling Abi their ancient jokes, like "What D'You Call a One-Eyed Dinosaur?".

* * *

16

By October the group had got into their stride. Each Friday all of them, apart from Llyr who was busy on the farm, arrived early. They practised singing "Kalinka" and dancing crouched on their heels like the Red Army, and when Ellen came they'd refuse to let her in till she uttered the password, "Stanislavsky". Then Spock on the keyboard would change from "Kalinka" to the Soviet national anthem and they'd stand to attention with a click of their heels. "Goose-step!" Ellen would bark, and they'd march up and down like guards at Lenin's Mausoleum in Red Square. Or "Georgian women!" and they'd glide along like dolls on wheels.

During the last week, Ellen got down to practicalities. "Warmth," she said. "In November it can go down to minus eighteen in Moscow – that's the temperature in a home freezer. But flats are centrally heated and very warm. No thermal undies, just layers of sweaters and coats. Now, presents. The Russians – I'm sorry, the Soviet people – are generous. We're rich, and we'll take them pens, tapes, tights and stockings, chocolates, soap – especially soap, there's a shortage. But I warn you, they'll shower you with books, ornaments, kettles, samovars, *balalaikas*... Tom?"

"Shouldn't we take them a harp?"

"Think of our baggage allowance – we'll have a keyboard, double bass, Mari's guitar – all our gear for the *Carousel* and *West Side Story* scenes..."

"Can we take our hair-driers?" asked Abi.

"Russian plugs have got different pins, sweetheart," said Tie, stretching his length out on

17

the floor. "And our multi-purpose plug is for keyboard and lights only." Spock nodded agreement. Tie Tighe and Spock Speakman were twin musical geniuses, and inseparable. Both were six foot tall with three earrings in each ear, but Tie spoke and Spock was silent.

"Russian language and culture. I'll prepare duplicated sheets with a list of words like *please* and *thank you*. Their school specializes in English, as you know, but you can make a small effort at Russian. I'll include some signs you'll come across, like *Gentlemen* and *Ladies*. They'll be in the Cyrillic alphabet... Finally – alcohol. Mr Gorbachev has put restrictions on alcohol sales, but people flout them all the time. Watch out for vodka, it's extremely potent. Anyone who ruins the trip by getting drunk will be banned from future visits. Understood?"

And we sit here, thought Megan, taking all this without a murmur. Coming from anyone but Ellen we'd be raising eyes to heaven. Is anyone else wondering what I'm wondering – what's in all this for her? Doesn't she fancy Griff any longer? (Mr Griffiths, Head of Maths, wildly good-looking and recently divorced.) Is she going for this Russian guy, Oleg? No one's even made puns on his name – talked about getting Oleg legless, or showing Oleg a leg.

No, Ellen should stick to Mr Griffiths, if she stuck to anyone. Though Megan couldn't imagine Ellen actually succumbing to the married state. She was too strong-minded.

* * *

18

Dafydd wasn't going to Moscow. Apart from music and Welsh, his passion was computers.

Megan had known Dafydd all her life. Her first memory of him was when she was four years old. Whenever Kate was rushed to hospital in the middle of the night, little Megan had to go next door to Dafydd's mother. "Make sure Mr Morgan's home and sober, Bill," Mummy would shout as Daddy ran downstairs. In the morning Dafydd's mother would tug a comb through Megan's red curls and nag them down the hill to the playgroup in the village hall. Dafydd's mum always nagged you one minute, mostly in Welsh, and cosseted you the next. His father was either shouting his head off, or in bed, drunk. What was "drunk"? Megan would speculate what kind of drink made you go like Mr Morgan. Orange juice, lemonade? Might it happen to anyone – to her? And how long before Mummy and Daddy got back, and might Kate have died?

On one of these crisis mornings, Megan was so frightened and angry that she wanted to upset everyone. She started with Dafydd's mum. Half-way down the foggy lane, she called out, "Need a wee. Need it *now*." She meant to force them to go back home so they'd miss the playgroup, but Mrs Morgan just led her to a gateway, turned their backs on Dafydd and exposed her bare bottom, undignified, to the cold. She hadn't been able to produce a trickle.

Megan hated the playgroup, which was run by Mrs Lloyd, a retired schoolmarm with sharp elbows and a sharp nose. That morning she hated

Mummy as well, and Daddy and Kate and... She didn't hate Dafydd, but Dafydd wasn't taking any notice of her – he was in the sand-pit burying little plastic people in the sand. She decided she'd run away.

She pretended to go to the toilets in the lobby, but she went past them and out of the heavy green door and along the street. It was raining. The raindrops were cold on her face. She was scared. A car came along the village street and splashed her, so she ran into an alley between two houses to hide. Panic! Maybe someone would come out and catch her and put her in prison! She'd have to go back. She crept out of the alley and started to walk miserably, dragging her feet. She was wet – Mrs Lloyd would see she was wet!

When she reached the heavy green door there was a head poking out of it, peering this way and that. It was Dafydd. "Where you been?" Dafydd knew English, but usually he'd only speak Welsh. If he spoke English it was an honour. "Yer wet." He took her hand and they went back in together.

Mrs Lloyd was in the far corner with her back turned. Dafydd led Megan to the water bowl, where he picked up a cup and a funnel and started to splash water over her. She splashed him back, and they laughed with glee and splashed till they were both soaking wet. Mrs Lloyd turned round. She ran over to screech in their faces, but the two of them didn't care. They just giggled, and the other children joined in. Mrs Lloyd had to clap her hands and announce "Juice time!", and Dafydd and Megan munched Rich Tea biscuits huddled together against the radiator to get dry.

Not long after that morning, Dafydd's mother left his father – left home – and the house next door was sold to the Haighs. Mr Morgan went into hospital in Chester ("As if that'll do him any good," said Megan's dad.) and Dafydd went to live in the next village with his *nain* and *taid*.

Dafydd and Megan went around together in a childish kind of way when they were eleven because everyone, except Dafydd, laughed at Megan in her hideous round specs and her all-over freckles.

When she was fifteen, she got herself set up with contact lenses and felt pretty again. She asked Dafydd to her birthday party, and they'd indulged in a brief spell of adolescent passion. But then Phil, an engineering student from the Tech, had arrived on the scene. "Dafydd? Who's Dafydd?" she'd said to Kate.

"Megan!" sighed Kate in exasperation. "It'd serve you right if someone mucked you about like that!"

Kate got her chance to say "I told you so". After Phil broke it off, Megan decided to give up men. She threw herself into Drama Club as if nothing else existed.

As they all planned and waited for Moscow during the first half of the autumn term, the atmosphere at home became almost contented. Kate didn't have a single asthma attack, even though she was heading for A-levels. Mum was anxious about Kate working too hard and about Megan's trip, but then she was always anxious. Megan didn't let herself get infected by it. When Mum begged, "You will phone from Moscow, darling?" she replied confidently, "I doubt it."

She wasn't even being nagged by Dad. Dad taught PE in Chester (plus Maths when they couldn't find anyone better qualified), and he'd at last been appointed Deputy Head. What's more, he'd begun to tolerate Kate's new boyfriend, Jason, and Kate gave the credit for that to Megan.

"It was him mending Spock's keyboard that did it, honestly," said Megan. Jason and his family were into rock music, and they ran an instrument repair business from home. This was one reason why Dad couldn't stand Jason – "I *know* these sort of people, I *teach* them, Kate" – and the other was that his arms were tattooed.

Dad and Kate had endless rows about it. Dad and Kate's rows were predictable but terrifying. Dad's temper would fly out of control and Kate would threaten to lose her breath. At this point Mum always started to cry, and Megan would panic and run to her room.

But this time Megan surprised herself by standing her ground and calming everyone down. What's more, she did it by coming in on Kate's side. "If Jason's so brilliant with electronics, maybe he could have a go at mending Spock's keyboard?" Dad was so surprised that he agreed, and feeling rather dazed they all sat down and had tea. Later that week Jason got to work on the keyboard, and he made it sound like new. Ellen came up to the cottage to thank the Shipways personally for finding the miracle-worker. So Dad relented: Kate could officially go out with Jason. And Kate and Megan were on friendlier terms than ever before.

It was the affair of the keyboard that brought Dafydd into Megan's life again. Dafydd played keyboard as well as guitar; he and his group often used the one in the studio. The Tuesday after Jason mended it, he came to try it out.

"Hi, Megan," he said, slightly puffed. He'd run over from the main building. It was raining, and he flicked rats' tails of wet hair off his face.

It wasn't that he'd grown. He was the same quiet, square-faced, brown-eyed Dafydd he'd always been. But to Megan he seemed steadier and more alert, less preoccupied with dark thoughts. She'd heard that his mother was back in Pentre. For years she'd only spent weekends with him and his grandparents because she could only get a job in Aberystwyth, but now she was living with them the whole time. Dafydd had gone out with Barb Shepherd for a few weeks but that was over now.

His "Hi, Megan" was as Welsh and musical as "Cwm Rhondda", but this time Megan didn't recoil. She grinned at him. "Hi, Dafydd. All right?"

"All right. Done a grand job on that keyboard, hasn't he? Where did you find him?"

"Kate's boyfriend," she said. "Does repairs for groups all over Merseyside and Deeside."

"Does he, then. Must see him about my guitar, if he's not too busy."

"You could come up to our place, maybe. Dad's given permission for him to enter the portals on

23

Sundays. You could catch him there – better than trailing over to Connah's Quay to the shop. Visit the haunts of your childhood." Was he still mad at her for throwing him over for Phil? She didn't care, she was just chatting on.

"I might do that, if I may."

"'If you may', Dafydd Morgan. Of course you may."

"Thanks," he said, blushing suddenly. "I will. But you're going off to Moscow soon, aren't you?"

"In two weeks' time."

"Would it be OK this Sunday?"

"Fine."

"All right then."

"All right. See you."

He hitched his school bag over his shoulder and hung it on one finger the way he always did, and put up his collar against the rain.

Abi accused Megan of not saying a single word all the way home. "You must be getting that flu bug!" she shouted as they got off the bus and dragged their coats over their heads. "Five people in the fourth year went down with it yesterday!"

Megan kicked a puddle at her and got soaking wet herself. She mustn't be ill, she *couldn't* be ill, not when the only thing that mattered in the whole world was the trip to Moscow. Though… Dafydd mattered, and he was coming to see her on Sunday. What was it about Dafydd? He'd always been there. So was he just a friend – good to have around – nothing more? Not if he could make her stomach contract like he was doing at the moment.

No, she realized, glancing in through the rain-splashed window of their cottage – what Dafydd did was to make her feel calm inside. He was sometimes dark and moody, but however he felt he didn't make out it was your fault. That made him special.

And was she special to him? It seemed she was. "The trouble with life," she complained to Mish the following week, "is that it's got no idea how to pace itself. First you get long miserable spaces of emptiness" – she meant, long spaces of trying to demonstrate that someone else existed in the world besides sickly Kate Shipway – "then everything falls over itself to happen at once."

"Why?" asked Mish. "What's happening besides Moscow?"

"Me and Dafydd," said Megan.

"Well, you and Dafydd will just have to wait, then, won't you?" said Mish.

CHAPTER TWO

*First he must see this one through, this new life,
then he could go back to the one that had been
interrupted.*

Pasternak, *Doctor Zhivago*

More than three hours in the air. Megan had only
flown once before, an hour's flight to Paris to
celebrate Kate's sixteenth birthday. These two
hundred minutes seemed like a day and a half.
"What, no in-flight movies?" demanded Abi. Her
parents, needing "peace and quiet, away from this
mob, thank you very much-a", were up at the
superior end of the plane.

During the last hour they all got a bit hysterical,
except Spock, who was deep in an article on the
World Cup Qualifier between Turkey and the
USSR. Megan was nervous. She was determined to
keep calm and not show off.

Abi, beside her, had been restless the whole time.
Now she was standing up and reading out the letter
she'd had from Nina, her Russian partner. "'I will
greet you with happiness upon your arrival in
Moscow. Her population is eight million persons
and it is necessary to remark that she has thirteen
hundred industrial enterprises...'" All the fifth
years except Spock and Jim rolled around in their

seats laughing. Gentle Mrs Garth Jones begged them just to "sit down in your seats – don't disturb the whole plane, please, dears."

Megan had to giggle with the others. She felt twinges of nausea. Surely the flight would soon be over? Maybe she should read them her letter from Riina? Riina sounded pleasant but incredibly old-fashioned. But Megan needed to like her. They had to get on – they'd got more than a week together. Friendship across international boundaries, it was a beautiful warm fantasy... Another nauseous twinge.

She had to stop herself staring at the paper sick-bag in the mesh pocket. Fumbling amongst the belongings under her seat, she found Riina's envelope.

"Hey, listen to this!" she called. "'Whereas I live in Moscow, my true country is Estonia, which nestles in the moody embrace of the Baltic Sea. My languages are Estonian and Russian, and also humbly English. But my vocabulary is very weak, and I crave your indulgence for my grammatical mistakes...'"

Meredydd and Tom collapsed into the aisle – "Embrace my indulgences!" – just as the stewardess with her drinks trolley was struggling back to her post. Vodka bottles collided, and paper cups spilt their sticky remains all over the carpet. The stewardess' black eyebrows shot into a single angry line. Mrs Garth Jones leapt up in distress. But Ellen appeared, and Mrs Garth Jones let her through.

"*Prostitye*," she said to the stewardess, and came out with several sentences of careful Russian.

27

She'd told them she didn't know any! She must have been labouring away with tapes in secret.

Ellen's efforts did the trick. The stewardess' black eyebrows unknitted, and all ended in smiles.

When the drinks trolley had disappeared back up the aisle, Ellen turned round and faced the group. Megan braced herself for a furious "Thank you, everyone..." with a death-ray from Ellen's laser eyes.

But there were no death-rays. She was almost gentle. "Listen," she said. "We're all very nervous. Yes, I am too. This could be a wonderful trip, or it could be a disaster. You've had these sweet puzzling letters from your partners, and you've no idea who's behind them. We've all been brought up on Cold War politics. But things are changing. Trips like ours might turn out to be just as important as all President Gorbachev's summit meetings."

Megan's nausea eased. The plane's nose shifted in a groundward direction. Soon they'd be landing.

"Oleg Baranov is a marvellous person," Ellen went on, "and the whole group's dying to meet you. Relax. In the end, we're only human, and if we make a few cock-ups, no doubt they'll let us off." She turned and went to sit down.

Riina's letter was still in Megan's hand. She took a deep breath and read the rest of it. "I like very much your song 'Scarborough Fair', but perhaps you will teach me also Welsh songs. My primary passion is for the drama, and I follow greatly the productions of our Moscow Students' Theatre..."

She caught Mish's eye over the aisle, and they both grinned.

The airport was dim and bare. No café or restaurant was to be seen – all signs were in the strange Cyrillic script. Megan felt tired and confused.

Mari and Annest got through Passport Control first and decided to go to the Ladies. A quarter of an hour later they came back. "One loo locked," they reported, "and the other's *filthy*!" At Customs there was a massive queue. Their group was wedged behind three businessmen loaded with boxes of electronic gadgets, every one of which had to be unsealed and meticulously examined.

Megan's eyes started to itch. She rubbed them impatiently. Then, "Help!" she shrieked. "I've lost one of my lenses! Don't move, anyone – it'll be down here somewhere…"

Everyone tried to keep still at the same time as moving around to hunt for the tiny sliver of transparent plastic. "What does it look like, Megan?"

"It doesn't look like anything – it's invisible!" God, if she'd lost it, she wouldn't be able to see anything the whole trip…

Then, as suddenly as she'd been blinded, she could see again. "I've got it! It was in my eye all the time – it'd just slipped out of place!"

Abi hit Megan over the head with a carrier-bag full of presents. Then Olwen said suddenly, "Look!" and pointed beyond the Customs counter. The dark glass barrier was the height of a person, and a crowd was standing behind. Tall young heads could be seen peering over the top. Then scarves and single carnations started waving in the air, and a few teenagers spilled through the forbidden doors and glanced tentatively in the direction of the Customs queue.

"It's them – it must be them!"

The ones who'd squeezed through disappeared behind the doors again. A banner shot above the barrier, held up on poles. It read: WELCOME TO MOSCOW, PENTRE CORACH FRIENDS!

No one knew what to do. "Where's Ellen?" Megan asked Olwen.

"I don't know – where is she?" The mutter went breathlessly round the group – "Where is she?"

Mish spotted her – she was on the far side of the concourse, waiting for the double bass and the keyboard to come through. Mish ran over like someone in training for the Olympics. In a few moments she was back, Ellen running behind her. Mish, suddenly shy, stood aside. Ellen slowed down to a walk and approached the doors.

A man came half-way through, and stopped. He held the door with his foot and put out a hand. Ellen walked towards him. It was Oleg Baranov.

Megan was taken aback. Oleg was slight, like Ellen, and about the same height. His face was narrow and thin and etched with lines like crevices on a mountainside. He was combing his fingers through his hair too but Ellen's hair was short and neat, whereas his looked as if it hadn't been brushed for a week.

But it was his eyes that shocked Megan. They

were large but deep-set, and they somehow looked alert and haggard at the same time – inspired and defeated.

No, Ellen couldn't possibly fancy Oleg Baranov. He was ancient, he must have been through several wives already, not to mention a lake full of vodka. Ellen was young – she couldn't, she wouldn't…

"Megan!" Abi was nudging her and pointing to the Soviet group. They'd lowered their welcome banner and were jumping up and down. There was a momentary glimpse of one face, then another. "Which d'you think's Nina? Or Riina? Nina and Riina! We'll have to go around in a foursome – see if we can get four of the fellas and make up a gang…"

"That's Riina." Megan nodded towards one end of the bouncing crowd. "The one in the blue woolly hat."

Abi was amazed. "How d'you know?"

"Fair hair, like the Scandinavians. She comes from up there, up north. Estonia."

Mrs Haigh ordered, "Wait, if you please," (Mr Haigh nodding lofty assent beside her) "until everyone is past Customs!"

"Right?" asked Ellen eventually. "Right."

Megan's heart turned over. It was like the catch-phrase between her and Dafydd – "All right? All right." What would happen if she fell for one of the boys waiting behind that barrier? She'd have to learn Russian. She was no good at languages, she'd messed around in Welsh and French lessons. For all her Welsh name, she was English and proud of

it, proud as Dafydd was to be Welsh. Fall for a
Russian? She was getting as bad as Abi! What
about Dafydd?

They were moving. Spock dragged the box with
the keyboard, Mari had her guitar over her
shoulder. Laden with baggage, the seventeen Brits
approached the barrier. The Russians held the
doors open. Megan felt their corner of the airport
suddenly become breathless.

For a second, both groups hardly dared look at
each other. The welcome banner hung limply; the
hosts clutched their carnations anxiously to their
chests.

Then Oleg gave a little mock bow. "Welcome
indeed, Miss Tudor-Williams! And a great
welcome to you all!"

"*Diolch yn fawr*," said Ellen. The Welsh gang
had threatened murder if she didn't speak at least
one Welsh phrase per day. "It's wonderful to be
here. Would you please make the introductions?"

This was the part Megan had been dreading.
Riina might be all right, but what about her
parents? The letters said her father was doing
scientific research, and her mother had been a
high-powered lawyer back in Estonia but could
only get work as a legal secretary in Moscow.
Megan, going a bit wild, had described her father
as an athlete, her mother as an artist and Kate as
an invalid.

Oleg took out a piece of paper and
ostentatiously cleared his throat. "The
partnerships," he announced. "This was for us a
procedure filled with anguish. Every girl and boy

from Pentre Corach seemed so delightful that each wished to be partner for each Pentre Corach. But finally, as you know, we made our decisions."

Abi started to giggle. Megan kicked the side of her foot.

"First, the young men. Keith." Spock stepped forward, looking more than ever like a flagpole. "Your friend, Sasha." A boy of about sixteen stepped out – very fair, very small. He peered up at Spock as they shook hands. Everyone laughed, including the boy's small parents.

"Thomas – Levan."

A tall, solid boy shook Tom's hand. "Levan is a Georgian name, I am from Georgia. Here is my mother and my grandmother." Megan had imagined every Russian *babushka* to be round, rosy and swathed in black. But Levan's *babushka* was tall and elegant in a fur-collared coat and four-inch stiletto heels, and his mother was twenty years younger and an exact replica.

"Meredydd – Seriozha. That is, Sergei," explained Oleg. "Seriozha is for, as you say, short." Laughter again. It's going to work, Megan thought – it's going to be all right... And there wasn't a single one of the lads who compared with Dafydd.

She concentrated on meeting Riina. Certain that Riina was the blue-hatted girl at the end of the crowd, she decided to will the eyes to meet hers. She set her gaze on the face with the fair hair, and stared.

It only took a couple of seconds to work. She'd just begun to take in the girl's appearance – sculptured nose and jaw-line, eyebrows so blonde you could hardly see them, neat figure in an old-fashioned waisted coat – when the small blue eyes darted across to hers.

Megan and the fair-haired girl grinned at each other across the space. I hope it *is* her, thought Megan. What if I'm lumbered with that amply upholstered female over there?

"Abigail – Nina." Megan took in a sharp breath. The amply-upholstered female was Abi's partner. The square face sliced itself in a smile, and a slab-like hand demanded to be shaken. Abi hesitated, then forced herself into motion. "Nina! How wonderful to meet you. May I introduce my parents?"

At last Megan's turn came. "Megan – Riina." Yes, it was the girl in the blue woolly hat.

Riina's eyes disappeared in laughter and the neat-waisted coat swayed as she strode across. Behind her came her mother, with the same strong bone structure as Riina's but shorter hair in warm brown curls, and her father, small and overweight with sausage-like fingers and an enormous grin. She was engulfed in carnations and kisses. "Most pleased – happy – wonderful" – words of welcome tumbled all over her.

She extracted herself eventually, and stood between Riina and her parents, looking round at the growing number of pairs. One glance made her blink with new eyes. Beside their Soviet partners, the Pentre Corach gang looked like a load of tramps from Waterloo Station. Tie's jeans – what was fashionably called "distressed" – were more rips than fabric, and Meredydd's green-and-orange striped trousers looked like pyjama bottoms. Mari, under her torn anorak, wore five baggy T-shirts one on top of the other. Only Gentleman Jim and Farmer Llyr looked half-way respectable.

"And finally, Michelle – Nadya."

Mish completed the tramp-portrait. Square and solid with spiky hair, clad in slit jeans and old trainers, she looked like the buffoon half of a comedy duo. The girl called Nadya, gliding towards Mish and standing like a ballerina, had her hair hanging glossy down her back and long sleek legs in unladdered tights. Megan wondered as they went out into the biting cold: so who's the poor relation?

It was getting dark by the time their bus lumbered round the Moscow Ring Road. Megan glanced alternately out of the window and at Riina beside her. She didn't know what to say, but she was relieved of making conversation by the guide giving a commentary at the front.

"My name is Sylvia, and I will be your Intourist guide for the tours of Moscow. I understand that the young people will wish to be with your families. Nevertheless, it is convenient to be led to all the historic places. Moscow, you understand, is a Hero City, for here Hitler was first defeated in the Great Patriotic War. However, we have many problems in our country. Now we discuss these problems freely, as a result of Mr Gorbachev's policy of *perestroika*..."

Megan looked at Sylvia's friendly, efficient face. Might Abi's mother be right? She'd declared that

all Intourist guides were spies employed by the
KGB. So too were hotel staff, especially the women
who sat on the landings and confiscated your key
every time you left the room. "Don't trust any of
them. They're watching your every move…"
They'd have a job to watch all us lot, Megan
concluded, when we're in our friends' flats or
theatre workshops. Unless Oleg Baranov and the
parents are all in the KGB too?

"Now we are coming near to the area where you
will be staying with your friends. As you can see, it
is a pleasant residential area with few industrial
enterprises. Many people wish to live here."

Pleasant? Megan gazed out of the window into
the dusk. But it's flats, flats, flats! Walls of them,
twenty or more storeys high. Every so often the
wall of flats would give way to a dark patch of
birch forest, then the glistening walls would start
yet again. No gardens, no parks, no little shopping
arcades anywhere to be seen. Each tiny window
was lit, with curtains undrawn, so it seemed there
was a Milky Way of millions of tiny people pressed
tight into a stiff rectangular space. Did Riina's
family live in one of these rabbit hutches, then?

Abi reached over to pull Megan's sleeve, and
jerked her head in Nina's direction. Nina had
turned her bulk round in her seat and was chatting
animatedly to Abi's parents behind. "We in Russia,
we love your Mrs Thatcher. She is so strong a
woman. She came to our country – she spoke on
television – she argued with our greatest TV man,
but she knocked him into little pieces!" Mrs Haigh
was looking positively mellow.

"Do a swap, then, shall we?" called Tom. "Your Mr Gorbachev for our Iron Lady? She's going a bit rusty, mind – wouldn't pass the MOT test…"

Megan turned to Riina. "Do you like our Mrs T, Riina?"

Riina's eyes twinkled. "I think politics is like a marsh, yes? A bog, where – slurp slurp, and you are gone! Me, I am mad for the theatre. You are mad for theatre too, Megan?"

"Crazy for it. Tell me what we're going to see."

"Megan, it will be wonderful! In this time you are here, the Moscow students produce their play – the so funny play called *Lysistrata*. Do you know this play?"

"Lice what?"

"It is Greek, it concerns… Oh, I cannot tell you, it is too funny. And the students there, they are so intelligent and brave and… But we will do dramatic workshops too, yes – with Oleg Stepanovich and Miss Tudor-Williams? Our drama – it is strong. And you will perform? We adore the English drama, Shakespeare, *Hamlet*. 'To be, or not to be: that is the question'!"

"We're not going to do Shakespeare – you're not expecting *Hamlet*, are you?" Oh God, thought Megan – what will they make of *Carousel*, a forty-year-old musical comedy in Welsh?

Ellen stood up at the front of the bus. "Pentre Corach – your attention please. The coach will soon be stopping to drop you off near your family's homes. The plan is this. We'll have sightseeing and educational trips each morning – for these the coach and Sylvia our guide will be available. In the afternoons we'll gather at the Studio Theatre for our drama workshops and presentations. In the evenings there'll be entertainment or social gatherings. Mr and Mrs Garth Jones, Mr and Mrs Haigh and I are staying at the Salyut Hotel. Any questions? Meredydd? In English, please, not Welsh."

"Ellen – erm – should we call you Miss Tudor-Williams while we're here, or what?" A nervous titter went up and down the bus.

Ellen gave a half-laugh and glanced down at Oleg Baranov. "Well – I don't know. I suppose... You ought to call the adults by their surnames, maybe..." Megan had never seen Ellen nervous like this.

Oleg Baranov stood up, his lank hair flopping over his forehead, a diagonal smile splitting his lined face. "But we are not children now. Surely, we are ambassadors! I am accustomed to be called Oleg Stepanovich by the pupils, but this form of address is strange to you. So – all may address me as Oleg. Then you also, Miss Tudor-Williams, may be called Ellen."

There was relieved laughter, and the bus drew up at the side of a wide avenue. Megan took her place in the aisle and filed with the rest of them out of the bus.

If (she thought) nothing works in the Soviet Union, as Mrs Haigh declared, then the lift won't work, and Riina's family are sure to live on the twentieth floor, and at the nineteenth her father will drop my suitcase down the stairs, and...

But the lift arrived, they all four squeezed in, and it slowly went up. Megan's main fear was that her fly-away hair would tickle Mr Tormis' bald pate. Nobody spoke. It was as if a spell had been cast on them between the Intourist coach and the apartment. They got out at the tenth floor and, after Mr Tormis had undone three separate locks, they went in and switched on the lights.

"Welcome!" The spell broke. Mr and Mrs Tormis and Riina seized both Megan's hands, and smiles flooded their faces.

Then Riina was offering Megan slippers for her feet. Of course – Ellen had warned them you had to take off your shoes at the door. The slippers were turquoise lurex with a puff of fur on the toe, the sort that Megan's great-aunt in Bournemouth might wear. Obediently she took off her heavy black lace-up shoes.

Riina looked up. "You have man's footwear? You do not like the stilettos?"

"No," said Megan. "This kind are in just now. No one our age wears stilettos." Oh – Riina was wearing high heels! "I'm sure they're the height of fashion over here…"

But Riina was anxious. "You have spent so lots of money on your holiday here – you have none left for the fashion…"

"No, truly, I chose these shoes, they cost me — "

Mr Tormis interrupted with an instruction to Riina in Russian – or was it Estonian? "Come, the kitchen," said Riina. "My mother has cooked many things, you must eat."

After eating three slices of a cake with

"Welcome to Moscow" on top, as well as sweet cakes, slices of cold meat and slabs of cream cheese, Megan didn't want another mouthful for the rest of the week. If this was Soviet food shortages, what was normal? They were so kind it was claustrophobic.

A small glossy tabby cat slithered through the kitchen door and made for Riina's knee. It lay purring confidently. "She's gorgeous!" said Megan. "What's her name? We've got a cat at home, she's just had three kittens and we've had such arguments about names for them all…"

"He is a he," said Riina. "My father needs a boy among his girlish family. I named him. His name is Kostya."

"Eat more cake, you must," insisted Mrs Tormis. "You travel far – need be strong for the visit."

At last Megan convinced them that all she needed was sleep. Now came the crunch: would she have a room – or even a bed – of her own?

They stood up from the table and Riina put down the cat. Kostya? The Shipway cat was called Moel, because she was a small mountain like Moel Famau. Just now, bedtime, she'd be carrying her kittens in her mouth back to their basket.

Home! Megan felt sprayed with loneliness as if from a shower in the ceiling. Home – Mum and Dad – they'd be lounging in front of a crackling fire – Dad would be traipsing out to the shed for logs because he couldn't nag Megan to go – Kate'd be upstairs squeaking away on her clarinet…

What if Kate had had an attack? She must

phone! She couldn't – it was only at 4 a.m. this morning that they'd waved her off on the coach to Heathrow. She mustn't panic. But if she could only hear a familiar voice – not necessarily her parents' – Mish's, Olwen's, Abi's even...

She followed Riina along the hall. What a tiny apartment! In the kitchen they'd only got a small plastic-topped table and four cheap chairs, but even so you had to squeeze to get between your chair and the cooker. Here was the sitting room, small, square and filled with old-fashioned furniture and academic books. The hall too was dark with books.

As Riina opened the bedroom door, Megan had a sudden thought. Her comb! She'd lent it to Abi back at Heathrow. She'd phone Abi and ask for it. She could phone her now, at what-was-her-name's – Nina's. She asked casually, "What time is it? Would it be too late to phone someone?"

"Telephone?" asked Riina. "Perhaps. But what is your need? If we can give you something —"

"No, it's just my comb. These ghastly curls of mine need a special comb, an Afro, and I lent it to Abi. Could I give her a ring at Nina's and say, bring it tomorrow?"

"Nina? But that is difficult. I have not her number, I am not with her a particular friend – "

"Could you look it up?" Why did Riina seem distressed? "I'm sorry, have I – is it...?"

"It is I to be sorry, Megan. We cannot look for a name. I learnt in our English Culture lessons, you have a volume where names are written —"

"The telephone directory."

41

" – directory, you find names if you wish to telephone. But in Moscow, in Soviet Union, we cannot acquire such a volume. It is a matter of security, they say."

No telephone directory? Megan was shocked. Maybe Abi's mum was right about the system. Maybe the phones didn't work like ours. Then how would she phone home if she needed to? Nine days – it felt as though she'd be away nine months!

Riina put out a hand. "You be tired. I am sorry. Here," she said. "We sleep here. You," she pointed to a sofa converted into a bed, – "and me," to a folding bed. Both had a kind of quilt spread on top.

"Lovely," Megan said, sounding artificial. "That'll be fine."

"I know," Riina said, forlornly pushing a strand of fair hair behind her ear. "You in England have special rooms where visitors may sleep. I wish we too. But it is not possible."

What about privacy? Would she ever get a moment to think, to write to Dafydd? "It's fine, great, honestly," she murmured lamely. She tried to smile, feeling it must look like a grimace.

"Tomorrow," said Riina, trying to cheer her up, "I will tell about everything – Estonia, the wonderful Moscow Students' Theatre, everything. And I will tell you…" She paused, grinning. "No, it will await the morning."

"No, now!" At last, here was something intriguing. "What is it? Don't keep me dangling in suspense – "

The grin spread upwards till Riina's eyes almost disappeared. "No, it is a slight thing, you cannot be curious. It is only a boy. Await tomorrow, please."

"A boy?" But there was something authoritative as well as joking about Riina, something that reminded Megan of Ellen. "OK, then. Tomorrow."

Riina showed her to the bathroom, where she had to fight with festoons of washing on lines overhead, not to mention the cat's food and milk and litter-bowl in the middle of the tiny square of cracked lino. Then she fell on to her sofa-bed and dropped off before Riina had even finished her stint in the bathroom. She slept without a break till Mrs Tormis called them in the morning.

CHAPTER THREE

*They presented their permits at the town gates and
were driving into Moscow...*

Tolstoy, *War and Peace*

Breakfast was enormous. But it was exactly the
same food as last night. Slabs of cold meat, wodges
of cream cheese, and all the sticky cakes that
Megan hadn't been able to face before. The bread
was good – white bread rather like slices of an
enormous French loaf, and a thick brown malty
kind with a rich healthy taste. Megan saw it all
through a short-sighted blur because Kostya the
cat had slid so lovingly round her ankles in the
bathroom that she couldn't concentrate to put in
her lenses.

Mr Tormis wasn't there: he'd disappeared off to
work while the girls were still asleep. Riina's
mother hovered over them, not eating but dashing
anxiously from table to fridge to sink as if world
peace depended on it.

Back in the bedroom, Riina bent towards the
mirror and carefully applied foundation, powder,
eyeliner, mascara and lipstick. Then she gestured
to Megan. "Please," she said, "be free. We have
time before we walk to the place of the coach."

"I don't actually wear make-up much," Megan told her. "But see what I do wear. Do you have these in the Soviet Union?" She took her tiny contact-lens jar out of her shoulder-bag, unscrewed the cap and held it up for Riina to see.

"There is nothing!" Riina's eyes crinkled in a grin. "You English, you undertake these practical jokes!"

"No, they're to put in my eyes instead of glasses." Riina looked fascinated. Megan balanced her lens on a finger-tip and aimed for her eyeball.

A tiny discomfort niggled at her: Ellen had warned them not to show off the material goods that the West had to offer. Well, she wasn't showing off, she was just explaining. And Riina had obviously despised her lace-up shoes as men's throw-outs. Just now she was taking care not to snag her fine tights, while Megan was flinging on old knitted ones with cobbled toes where she'd mended them.

It was a grey day, bitterly cold. The two of them walked briskly along the pavement towards the meeting place with the wind whipping round their faces.

In the morning light the huge walls of flats looked colder and even more forbidding. The blocks hardly varied at all in design; they didn't announce "Here's home" so much as "Here's a fortress". An occasional small car park was scattered with a few dirty Moskvas, and the children's playground was deserted except for a lonely old man walking his dog. The only trees were a few rowans waving leafless twigs with stubborn bunches of red berries on the end.

"Riina," – Megan had to smarten her pace to keep up – "you said, last night – about the Students' Theatre – you'd tell me about a boy?"

"Oh?" Riina turned and grinned. "Did I tell something about a boy? About my English, Megan – you must inform to me about new words and idioms."

"Your English is brilliant. What about this boy, then?"

"There are many boys. Men. They are almost men, they are eighteen and nineteen. They cannot interest themselves in me, they cannot."

"But one of them *is* interested! Tell me, Riina!"

"His name is Kostya."

"That's the cat!"

"Why do you suppose I so named the cat?"

"Kostya! Is he good-looking? Is he fun?"

"Does he look handsome? Well... Fun? Yes, yes, yes. Everyone loves Kostya. No, that is untrue. His director, Ivan – Vanya, he is angry with him, because Kostya makes fun, makes jokes – "

"Sends up, takes the mickey, takes the michael, makes a monkey..."

"Megan, stop!"

"You said I must improve your English. Go on, he sounds terrific. Is he your boyfriend, then?"

"No. But..."

"Not yet, he isn't."

"Not – yet." But they were approaching the edifice of the Salyut Hotel ("for foreign visitors only") with the Pentre Corach and Moscow gangs waiting outside, and she suddenly became serious,

46

long-faced Riina again, concentrating on the dusty
pavement at their feet.

Abi stood in the middle of the gang, half hidden by
the square bulk which was Nina. She saw Megan,
held up her Afro comb and waved it over Nina's
head with a screwed-up look of despair. Mr and
Mrs Haigh and the Garth Joneses were standing in
one huddle, Ellen and Oleg Baranov and Sylvia the
guide in another. The Intourist coach was waiting
for them, but there was some hitch in proceedings.
Megan got within listening distance of Ellen and
tried to make out what was going on.

"But that's impossible!" (Ellen.)

"Nothing is impossible, Ellen." (Oleg.) "In our
Soviet Union, I tell you, there is no such thing as a
step. There is only a *leap*." He looked scruffier
than ever, a miniature Hunchback of Red Square.
He was smoking restlessly, his face registering fury,
irony and amusement.

"I explain." (Sylvia, with pained patience.) "It
is only for tourism. With commerce, all remains
the same."

"But one to *ten*!" (Ellen, her fine hair standing
up on end.) "When five minutes ago it was one to
one!"

Sylvia, firmly, "I will announce to the group.
Then perhaps it will become clear." She called
everyone to attention. "Ladies and gentlemen.
Important currency changes have recently been
enacted by our government. As you will know, our
money is the rouble. Until now the exchange rate
has been one rouble to one pound. Easy for you,

no problem. But many people in the streets were giving many more roubles for your pound. The problem is always the black market. So our government made the change, that one pound will now buy ten roubles."

A gasp went up. Ten roubles! The quicker minds realized what this meant for souvenir-hunting. Ten times as many roubles – ten times as much to spend in the Moscow shops...

"This new rate is for tourists only. All commerce and trade will remain at the previous rate. Do you now have questions on this matter?"

"Excuse me, yes." Gentleman Jim spoke up. The Pentre Corach gang turned round in surprise. "Does this mean that ordinary Russians, I'm sorry, Soviet people, will have to give ten roubles for every pound sterling?"

"It does. When I tell you that we have problems, I mean it truly. You will learn this. But I hope that your trip will be an excellent one also. Today," she went back to her usual tone of efficient boredom, "we visit the centre of Moscow, Red Square and our department store GUM. You will see also our proud achievement, the Moscow Metro. First, Miss Tudor-Williams will, if everyone gives her five pounds, change this into roubles at the bank in the hotel. There are one hundred kopeks to one rouble, and the Metro will cost you just five kopeks..."

Abi shoved Nina into the seat over the aisle from Megan, squeezed in beside her and, as the coach jerked into motion, leaned over with the Afro comb. "How's it going?" she asked in a stage whisper.

Megan, embarrassed in case Riina or Nina should hear, answered in a low voice, "Fine. You?"

Abi let the corners of her mouth droop down her chin. "Wonderful. Great. Brilliant."

Megan frowned and turned back to Riina. "Your roads are so wide – I'd be terrified to cross them!"

"Not each Moscow roads is so. This is new Moscow. After the war, you remember, was a great housing lack. They must build, build, build. So they build on new spaces and make wide roads."

"Remember – the war? But my parents don't even remember it!"

"Your teachers inform you, certainly? The war, it is the most important, the time most full of change for all our countries."

"Yeah, but..."

Abi lent over. "War's just history, isn't it? I mean, it's the nuclear thing now, isn't it, or the environment or something."

Nina faced them. "The Great Patriotic War informs us what we need to know: that world peace must be maintained at every cost. The Soviet Union must for ever be inviolate." She spat out the syllables "in-vi-o-late" like pistol shots.

Riina didn't argue. Turning her face back to the window, she murmured something Megan couldn't catch. "I didn't hear – ?"

"In my country," she said, addressing the window-pane, "we do not forget, neither. My country was taken, occupied – and we remember for ever. In this region of Moscow" – turning back to Megan, changing her tone and speaking at twice the volume – "we find the University. The building... Ah, the guide will tell."

Sylvia at the front was starting her spiel. "On your left soon you will see the University. There are seven such buildings in the same style, built by Stalin, our leader during the war. About Stalin we now learn terrible things, how he made many hundreds and thousands to suffer – maybe millions of people..." Megan glanced at Riina. Did the Estonians suffer under Stalin? Maybe even her parents? But Riina's face had gone blank again.

They drove on towards the centre of the city, with modern skyscrapers giving way to older, smaller buildings as elegant as London or Paris. "The Lenin Hills, overlooking the Moskva River," Sylvia went on. "From this place next Tuesday, on the evening after the Revolution Parade, you will come to watch the great display of fireworks. And see the Stadium in which the Olympic Games were held in the year 1980."

Megan tried to remember 1980. Nine years ago – she'd have been seven, just going from infants into juniors. Dafydd's gran brought him on a visit. She said his mum had come back for a while but then gone again because there were no jobs round Pentre...

"Soon, we make a small detour," Sylvia went on, "in order to show you the house of our great writer Leo Tolstoy."

Nina was quizzing Abi about the works of "the English writer" Charles Dickens. Which was her favourite, *Great Expectations* or *The Old Curiosity Shop*? "For myself I am captivated by the invigoration of *A Tale of Two Cities.*"

Abi said, "Dickens is OK – I haven't read much – he's a bit long-winded, isn't he? I'm keen on Jeffrey Archer, actually."

"Oh?" asked Nina. "Is he an important writer for England? Has he perhaps gained the Nobel Prize?"

Over a massive ring road, past numerous museums, and at last they could see the Kremlin with its golden cathedral domes.

There was no sunshine, so the domes didn't sparkle as Ellen had described them. But Megan was struck by their fairy-tale, other-worldly quality. Here was everything they'd seen in the brochures – the red crenellated Kremlin Wall with stars on each of their corner towers, the tall onion-topped towers filled with holy icons that Lenin and Stalin had forbidden the people to worship, the Communist headquarters where Gorbachev was blowing the old secrecy away. Or was he? Was everything just as secretive and repressive as it had always been? Would she find out – did she want to find out? Was she out to have a good time like Abi, or did she really want to get into the politics swamp?

They lurched in their seats. The coach was swinging round to skirt the grey river, then it turned again by one of the Kremlin towers and in a few moments they parked within walking distance of Red Square.

* * *

"Incident in Red Square." Megan could see the item in the *North Wales Advertiser*. "Fiery Megan of Clwyd braved the Kremlin yesterday when by accident she took a forbidden door into the Communist fortress – " Maybe Dafydd would read it and fly over to make sure she was all right...

But nothing happened to Megan. It was Gentleman Jim in his Reeboks and neat jeans who was mobbed by black marketeers, and they were all nearly run over by a black limousine filled with faceless politicians.

Moscow was getting all set up for the Revolution Parade on Tuesday. Along the main roads people had been putting up red flags, and here in the centre Lenin's portrait was draped over all the buildings. Riina translated some of the meaningless slogans, like "Welcome to the Great October". ("But it's November!" complained Megan, till Mish explained that they'd changed the calendar since 1917.) At St Basil's Cathedral they could see men rigging up TV lighting, and the Kremlin Wall was hung with banners from the different Soviet Republics.

The accosting of Jim by "representatives of the alternative economy" was a subtle affair. Megan and Mish watched from a distance.

It was clear that Jim hadn't a clue what was going on. A couple of young men, or a group of three or four, would wander casually up to him, separate him from the rest and say something friendly in broken English. Jim, being Jim, would smile and chat as if to prove to Mrs Haigh that Communists were decent people after all. Then the

Russians would lean closer and take out a bundle
of notes. Jim, shocked to the marrow, would
tighten his lips and, half guilty and half smug,
saunter self-consciously back to the group. In a
couple of minutes the process would start over
again.

Megan could see that most of their own
Russians thought it was hilarious. But Dima, Jim's
partner, was embarrassed, and dragged him away
from his fourth encounter to take a closer look at
St Basil's.

No, Megan thought, there was nothing to fear
from these Moscow boys. Not one could make her
heart flutter. They were all so young and spotty.
(How had Dafydd managed to avoid acne?)
Though Vitya, with his dark curls, a childlike gap
between his front teeth and a man's broad
shoulders, was quite attractive. So was Levan, the
tall Georgian, who seemed to be hanging round
Annest.

Vitya was obviously the leader. When the Brits
stood gobsmacked at the cobbled vastness of Red
Square, crawling with tourists and not a vehicle in
sight, Vitya lined everyone up for photographs.
"Point every person's rear towards St Basil's!" he
called. "Llyr – " (he pronounced it *Clear*) "you are
an elephant. Do not obscure the small lady!" Mish,
the small lady referred to, gave Llyr a kick from
behind and struck a pose.

It was then that the black limousine swept by.
Vitya had taken a photo, then Nina took one, then
the Brits poured out of formation to take theirs.
They were quarrelling amicably – "Get back to

your place – I was first! – no, you weren't, you pushy Welsh brute – " when two young policemen in smart grey uniforms marched towards them, indicating with their truncheons that the group should get out of the way smartish. Vitya and Levan started arguing in such spitting Russian that Megan was scared they'd get themselves arrested. But no, the shouts melted inexplicably into smiles, and Vitya and Levan shepherded the party away. "Our President has a visitor who must not be delayed!"

Oleg and Ellen, who'd been talking with the Haighs and the Garth Joneses near the Mausoleum, came over to see what was happening. They were just in time to be waved aside by two other policemen. Ellen and Oleg were deep in talk, and Megan heard Oleg saying, "It is possible that it is he. He is due to arrive at any moment now."

"But what answer can he give?" asked Ellen. "Hundreds of thousands – the whole place'll simply collapse!"

It took only a second for the black limo to flash past and disappear through the high red-brick arch in the Kremlin Wall. They watched it in silence. But Oleg had peered in through the shaded windows. "It is he, it is he!"

Olwen asked, "Who, Oleg?"

"I think it is the leader of East Germany. They have problems there, have you read this? Many people leave the country. They are pulled there, as iron is pulled to a magnet, by the wealth of the capitalist West —"

"And," broke in Ellen, "lots of them have got family in the West."

"The Government seeks to prevent them," Oleg went on. "They must not let them go. The leader – his decisions are nearly impossible. He 'walks through a storm', eh, Ellen?"

That was all the trigger the Welsh group needed. They burst into song. "*Pan fo'r storm – yn ei grym,*" began Tom, and the five others joined in like the chorus in grand opera – "*Paid ac ofni dim*". Then the English six took it up. "And don't – be afraid – of the dark… At the end – of the storm – Is a golden sky – And the sweet silver song of the lark…"

By the time they reached, "And you'll ne-ver – walk – a-lone", crowds had gathered and were gazing open-mouthed. Women in high-heeled boots, children in woolly hats with SKI or SPORT knitted in, young men in thick coats, old men with beer bellies – all of them stared amazed at this mad gang from North Wales singing their hearts out in two different languages and making gestures with their feet as if it all had something to do with football.

Megan, singing as lustily as the rest, was speculating in the back of her mind about Ellen. Oleg had said "He walks through a storm" as if it were a secret code between them. What about Griff? Half of the Bryn Corach sixth year sighed their hearts out because they thought Griff was going out with Ellen.

The song was over. "Look at that lot," Mish murmured to Megan. In a huddle a few metres away, Tom and Meredydd and Mari and Annest were chatting away in Welsh and posturing as if they were practising a satirical sketch. "*Pa faint*" was the only phrase that Megan could catch. She knew it meant "How much?" They were making fun of Jim.

Jim remained in his own little world, deaf to insults. But Megan was furious at the way the Welsh lot could exclude the English by switching language. And the English couldn't pay them back. "Learn Welsh, then," they'd taunt. "What do you do in Welsh classes, fall asleep?" Megan nearly marched over to tell them off.

But Sylvia was acting sheep-dog and rounding them up because it was time to go on the Moscow Metro, and then after a packed lunch they would visit Moscow's famous department store, GUM.

Moscow's Metro stations might look like a cross between Buckingham Palace and the National Gallery, but what took the Pentre Corach breath away was something quite different. "But – there's no *litter*! No *graffiti* on the *walls*!"

Sylvia smiled a weary smile. "From Britain, that is every person's comment. From Germany, they love the ceramic designs, the chandeliers, they do not notice that it is clean. But Britain is the capital of the world for litter, yes? And your written conversations on the public walls, they are famous everywhere."

"I thought we were going shopping," said Abi.

"We are," replied Sylvia. "Now you will see our renowned GUM." She waved at a huge building that looked as if it had a precinct of shops inside.

The group agreed to separate into pairs and meet twenty minutes later at the entrance. Megan and Riina set off, Megan feeling rich with roubles. "I'm thinking of earrings for Mum, maybe a big silky scarf for Kate. What can I get for Dad? Men are the end for presents, aren't they?" Riina strode ahead to open the door and didn't reply.

Inside, the store was a crush of people. It was worse than Pentre's Tesco on a Saturday. But what had they all come for? GUM wasn't separate shops, or a single store – it was a series of stalls. Some of the stalls were empty. Others had goods on just one shelf, or two if you were lucky. Not one was jam-packed with goods like Megan had expected. She'd wanted to browse along shop windows, but there were none.

And the presentation! There was no colour, no style. Odd items were scattered on bare boards. Megan's eye fell on a handbag lying alone on a shelf, a black patent leather one with a cheap chrome clip. It looked exactly like a handbag she'd seen at the jumble sale in aid of school drama equipment. No one had wanted it, even at thirty pence, and in the end Abi's mum threw it in a bin-bag with the remains of some corned beef sandwiches.

But – she would be polite. At the shoe stall she asked Riina about the prices and tried to compare them with British ones. At the knitwear stall, hung with garments even her great-aunt in Bournemouth wouldn't be seen dead in, she said, "Some of these are really pretty."

How was she going to buy presents? The only

possibility was a black Russian-spy hat for Kate. "How much is this one?" she asked. Riina looked inside the braid ribbon. "Seventeen roubles."

"One pound seventy! That's cheap!"

"But ask how much for us," said Riina.

Megan kicked herself. "Sorry. For a Russian, seventeen pounds. Rather expensive."

Riina turned abruptly and stalked off into the crowd. Megan hurried after. "Sorry, Riina. I know it's not fair..."

But Riina stopped, turned to face Megan and said in a low voice, "Megan, I must ask of you. Never call to me a Russian."

"Never call to...? Oh – I said 'Russian', I should have said 'Soviet people'!"

Riina's voice dropped even lower. "I am not a Soviet people. I am not a Russian people. I am a Estonian people." She walked on quickly, elbowing her way through the crowds.

Megan followed her, trying to keep up. It was like being told off by Teacher. She wanted to bite back – "Come off it, it's not that important, it's only like being Welsh!" – but she didn't know Riina well enough yet.

But what if it was worse than being Welsh? Wales had never been occupied by Stalin. "Riina –" She looked ahead. No swinging blonde hair, no neat-waisted coat. Only a jostle of strange seething masses.

God, where was Riina? Had she lost her – was she abandoned in the swarming throngs of bloody GUM...?

"Megan!"

An arm caught hers – Riina. They could only have been separated for a couple of seconds.

"I am so sorry. I am rude. I will later tell. Perhaps, if we be lucky, you and I may go to Students' Theatre. Then I will to you explain. But now is no time. We must purchase the hat, then discover the others at the doors."

On the bus back to the hotel, Olwen asked more about the man they'd seen being whisked through Red Square in the limo. Ellen said, "He's called Egon Krenz – he's just taken over from the hard-line Communist boss – "

"Honecker," said Oleg.

"A really nasty piece of work, Honecker was. Krenz is a Communist too – a slightly softer one. We don't know why he's flown to Moscow at this crucial point, but we suspect that – "

"If he is a sensible man – "

"He's seeking Gorbachev's backing for reforms."

"On the other hand," Oleg went on, "if he is *not* a sensible man – "

"He may be warning Gorbachev that he's got to shut the border tight, and clamp down on anyone who disagrees with him. Which is ninety-eight per cent of the population of East Germany," finished Ellen.

"Ninety-nine," corrected Oleg. The two of them were doing a magnificent double act. "Therefore 'fraternal aid' might be requested. Which, being interpreted, means invasion by tanks. It is nearly thirty years – thirty years, twice the time you have in your whole life! – since that Wall, that – " he suppressed a swear word – "Berlin Wall was made. Since that day, friends – families – are split in two. How can it be thus? In that country – in this country, too, in the time of Stalin – thus is how it is."

"Oleg..." began Ellen, and she broke into Russian. Slow and painful, but it was Russian. It excluded them as surely as Welsh excluded the English.

Meredydd was the first to get irritated. "It's not fair, Ellen. You promised not to make plans without consulting us."

"Not fair, is it," Abi put in, "to talk in a language we can't understand?"

Ellen said, "I'm sorry. I was asking Oleg what he'd got planned for our drama workshop tomorrow. He said we might start with getting-to-know-you games, and I said surely we can get through those quickly enough. After that, couldn't we do an improvisation of the night of the Berlin Wall?"

Hurrahs greeted that suggestion. Megan glanced at Abi: even she seemed eager for this history lesson. Then they separated to go to their own families for the evening.

Megan's evening was an uncomfortable one, making attempts at conversation with the Tormis parents despite their problems with English. Mr Tormis tried to tell her about the glories of Estonia, using phrases like "Finno-Ugric land people" and "waving with modest cornflowers"which he must have learnt from a guidebook. Eventually they turned on the TV. It was heavy classical music, and Megan fought back yawns.

As they went to bed, Riina told Megan that she'd persuaded Oleg and Ellen to excuse them from the folk concert tomorrow evening.

"It is most fatiguing, Megan – merely men from the army singing 'Kalinka' and women from Georgia moving like the dead dolls. Nadya is excused too, and her partner Michelle, who is also your friend, yes?"

"So where will we be going instead?"

"They graciously allow us," Riina said smiling, "to attend my most favourite place, the Students' Theatre."

CHAPTER FOUR

An actor lives, weeps and laughs on stage, and all the while he is watching his own tears and smiles.

Stanislavsky, *An Actor Prepares*

The studio where they were to have their drama workshops turned out to be a little converted shop at the bottom of a block of flats, not far from Riina's. Oleg said it was an experimental theatre, and the director was a friend of his and let him use it in the daytime. The walls and ceilings were painted black, the seats were wooden and piled up around the walls, the floor was black too and there was no proper stage.

"There!" Oleg swung his arms round in pride. "Our Studio Theatre!"

Shabby, thought Megan, but I suppose it'll do.

The Moscow girls were now all kitted out in neat leotards, the Brits in loose T-shirts and ragged jeans.

"Great," said Ellen. "Stand in a circle, everyone. Oleg, will you begin?"

"Take off every shoe, if you please, and throw them away!" Off came their shoes, to be thrown against a pile of chairs.

"I think you do not yet know every person's name. That is wrong and must be corrected. Vitya,

62

your socks, please." Vitya took no notice. Oleg shouted at him in Russian. Vitya leapt to attention, pulled his socks off and rolled them into a ball. "Mari!" called Oleg.

Vitya threw the socks to Mari. Mari, still confused, caught them but didn't know what to do next. Tanya called, "Shout 'Tanya' and throw!" The penny dropped. The socks flew from Mari to Tanya, Tanya to Spock (everyone seemed to know silent Spock by now) – then to Seriozha, then Meredydd, from Levan to Annest, from Mish to Nadya... At last Megan thought she must know every name in the group – though when they stood breathless round Ellen and Oleg again, she was still wondering, "Is it Mike who comes from Ukraine, or Levan? Is Masha twinned with Olwen, or is that Sonya?"

"Ladies and gentlemen," said Oleg. They fell instantly silent. "Sit. In a circle. Sit alternate – Russian, Welsh, Russian, English, Georgian, Welsh. It is not a tidy circle! Seriozha – come in a little."

He looked slowly round. Everyone was alert and tense. Megan noticed his hands – thin, bony and mobile. You could see the tendons flex as he gestured, and there was an old white scar beside the thumb of his left hand. Abi was sitting next to him; Megan had never seen her giving anyone such total attention.

"Now we are almost friends," he said. "We see each other, we smile, we call each by name. But there is more. We must *feel*." There was complete quiet in the dark bare room. "Take hands. Close all eyes. Concentrate. Our great director Stanislavsky said, 'Concentration is necessary, if you are to possess real feelings.'"

They closed their eyes. Megan could picture Seriozha sitting next to her, his shy uncertain eyes, his pock-marked skin. Her stomach rumbled. Nothing happened.

She was just about to open her eyes when she felt a squeeze of her right hand from Seriozha. What should she do? Ah! – pass it on. She squeezed Masha's hand with her left.

Suddenly, someone broke the silence: a deep voice, speaking in Russian. Megan opened her eyes. Levan.

"In English, please, Levan," said Oleg. "Or perhaps Georgian, then we might all understand." Titters round the circle.

"It is not right," said Levan, speaking steadily to Oleg. "It is not real. We do not truly feel."

They stared. What did he mean? Was this "the Russian soul" – or the Georgian soul? Oleg's eyes glinted, but his voice stayed casual. "*Spassibo*, Levan. Thank you. You will learn to feel. Continue – eyes closed."

Megan fluttered her eyes semi-closed. Levan went on staring at Oleg. "What do we feeling?" he asked. "Feeling strong, are we? Safe? Or is it weakness we feeling?" He was like a young stag locking horns with the pack leader.

"At this moment," Oleg's voice dropped to a lower register, as if in warning, "we try to feel modest, and a little hopeful. Eyes – closed – now."

Would Levan obey? Megan wanted to make

sure he shut his eyes before she did, but didn't dare. There was a breathless pause. Then the hand-squeeze came round again. Megan relaxed. An even shorter pause, and it came again – and again – and, quickly, again.

"Right!" ordered Ellen, taking over. "Stand!"

"Stand!" echoed Oleg.

"Thank you, Oleg." Now it was Oleg who got a ray from Ellen's laser eyes. "Moscow – touch your toes! Pentre Corach – leap-frog!" For the next ten minutes she had them climbing all over each other, catching the other's handstands, getting together with different partners and twisting themselves into complex knots. By the end, Megan knew that she'd tangled with every single person in the room. That was Ellen's aim – to get them laughing and easy with each other, so that the drama workshop proper could begin.

When she sat down on her sofa-bed later to write to Dafydd, she described Riina and the Tormises and the flat and the Moscow gang and Red Square and GUM, but she couldn't think how to describe the workshop about the Berlin Wall.

She sat with pen poised, listening to sounds of Riina and her mother in the kitchen preparing the evening meal. Would it be the same food yet again? After visiting not one, but two art galleries in the morning, they'd had lunch at a place they called a "House of Culture" in some nearby suburb. It was a buffet: the usual two varieties of bread, triangles of a processed cheese and some cold meat, a kind of coleslaw and slices of pickled beetroot.

Then the Berlin workshop. How to give Dafydd the flavour of it?

She scribbled a bit more, telling him that Riina's family had given her a proper set of Russian dolls and been ecstatic about Mum's drawing of the whole Shipway family plus cat and kittens. Then she sat back, closed her eyes and conjured up the workshop.

Ellen had sketched in the background. How the capital, Berlin, had finished the war in Russian-occupied Germany, how it had been split between West and East, and how lots of East Germans, hating life under Soviet-style Communism, fled to the West.

"But, Dafydd," wrote Megan, "it all sounds dull and historical when I write it like that. The thing is – to Ellen and Oleg, it was *real*. And to Riina and the others – even though they're our age, it's real to them too. I suppose they know what 'living under Soviet-style Communism' is like! On the way home, Riina admitted that they find the stuff about Stalin boring – they *know* Stalin was ghastly, they just want to get on and change things *now*. But think – when Mrs T. first arrived, Brezhnev was still in power and no one could twitch without the Secret Police scribbling it in their file! Gorbachev's not just different the way Thatcher's different from Kinnock – he's different like sunshine's different from rain.

"So – Berlin. Oleg divided us into two groups and told us each to get on with ordinary life – eating, sleeping, working. Ellen came to our half and gave us a few screwed up bits of paper hankie for food, and *two* chairs to sit on – between *twelve* of us. Then she went to the other lot and gave them lots of bits of paper hankie and *fifteen* chairs for those twelve to sit on! We were poor, and they were filthy rich.

"Oleg was on guard. He carried a chair-leg like a gun and patrolled up and down between the two groups. His job was to stop us poor ones getting over to where that rich lot were living.

"It was Vitya who first decided to make it over the border. Every so often Oleg would go off – I suppose even guards have to go to the loo. Vitya beckoned to the rest of us (of course we were all miming) and took us to look over at the other side. Then he made signals that we were to go back to work – and just before Oleg got back, Vitya had hopped it to the far side. (It's amazing how real that boundary was.)

"We got on as if nothing had happened – but next time Oleg went off, Meredydd and Seriozha and Sonya hopped over. Of course, Oleg started to notice. He pointed his gun at us, but we didn't care.

"Next time it was Mish and Nadya. (Guess who slaved away without budging? Yes – Nina!) When Oleg got back he was livid. He paced up and down and waved his gun at us. Then he went off – and just when Riina and I were going to do our hop, he came back at a run. So we pretended to carry on shifting coal.

"He went and turned down the lights, so we got the message and lay down to sleep. Ever so quietly, he got one chair after another and put them along the invisible boundary. The Berlin Wall.

"Then he put the lights on again, and we got up. When we saw the chairs, we went mad. We were trapped on our side – no more of us could get over! He aimed his gun at us, threateningly. We waved to the ones on the other side and they waved back.

"Oleg went off again, and Riina and I decided we'd make a run for it – try and get over the chairs. We set off – and straight away Oleg came running back. He shot us, and we fell where we were, over the chairs.

"Annest and Mari pulled me (my dead body) back over to our side, and Riina was pulled over by the other side. They were nearly in tears. Sasha really was crying. (Do Russian men cry more easily than you lot?)

"They gave us funeral services, at the same time on both sides, and the Russians (I mean – you know what I mean) hummed some tune that sounded like a religious service. I think I played dead pretty well – I tried not to move a single muscle.

"I've never been shot before, Dafydd, not even in a drama workshop. Shot, because of that bloody Wall... It brings it home to you, it really does.

" – Must dash – will write more tomorrow. Riina's just popped her head round the door to say 'Eat'. Tonight she and I and Mish and Nadya are sneaking off to watch some students rehearse this weird Greek play."

"Tell me about Kostya, then," demanded Megan. She and Riina had wrapped up warm, and Megan had tucked all her hair inside the yellow felt hat that she'd found in an Oxfam shop. The rest of her outfit was black: black T-shirt, black ribbed sweater, and her thick black cardigan that flopped down below her black jacket with the sleeves drooping over her hands.

"Kostya? He is so funny, Megan! But he is not truly happy. He is like the circus man, what is his name? The man who, if he did not laugh, he would weep? Clown! That is Kostya. He speaks not of his family, his home, he speaks not of his studies, his life is only for the theatre – "

"What does he study? Does he fancy you?"

"He studies law, as also does his friend Yuri. What is 'fancy'?"

"Um … find you attractive, want to be with you all the time, that sort of thing."

"Kostya … fancies, do you say 'he fancies'?"

"Yes. Why do all your men's names sound like women's names?"

"I do not understand?"

"Kostya – Vitya – Sasha – they all end in 'a'. Forget it. He fancies – ?"

"First he fancies with a girl, then he fancies with another girl – "

"Not fancies *with*, just *fancies* a girl."

"Then he *fancies* a different girl. But, last week, I arrived to see rehearsals, and … I cannot describe to you, Megan, he made me such happiness – and in the same moment also such pain…"

But she broke off. They'd reached the Metro station and Mish and Nadya were walking towards them. Mish had her enormous moonboots on and a thick hand-knitted scarf against the cold. Nadya was elegant as ever, but looked different in

69

a way Megan couldn't quite put her finger on, till she looked down and saw under Nadya's long woollen coat ... jeans. Not ordinary jeans, but snow-washed like the ones that had just gone out of fashion in Britain.

"Now we have freedom in Moscow!" Nadya twirled around and gathered them together like a leader with her team. Megan had hardly heard her speak a word so far, and thought what a boring week Mish would have. But this was a new Nadya. "How good to be separate from the many! Dima, Tanya, Sonya – they are like insects, they always be together, like childs. Me, I like to be with grown people. Come!"

They went into the Metro station, down some steps, past stout headscarved women selling carnations and change machines that coughed out five-kopek pieces in return for a ten or a twenty. "Walk to the right," Nadya reminded them as the two Brits kept bumping into people.

This station was at the end of the line, and a train was waiting. Nadya chatted away as they got on and sat down. "You have Metro in London, you call it Tube? I will go to London one day. You hear rock bands in London? You hear Uriah Heap? Uriah Heap came here, Moscow, two years ago –"

They sat down, two opposite two, and Mish leaned forward and explained that Uriah Heap was out now. Had she heard of U2?

"Me too?"

"No – *U-2* – they're a rock band..."

The train set off, and the noise made it even more difficult to communicate. As they approached

70

each station the lights flickered and a disembodied voice barked at them in Russian.

By the time they reached Prospekt Marxa Megan had picked up plenty of bits and pieces about Nadya. She wanted to be a rock singer in London or New York, she fancied most of the student actors but she wasn't going to let love stand in the way of her career. She thought *perestroika* wouldn't work till Gorbachev got rid of the black market, and all black marketeers should be lined up against a wall and shot. But she'd managed to get hold of a broken-down video recorder, some old Beatles records, some cassettes of just-out-of-date rock music and a music centre, not to mention her jeans – all from the West, and all on the black market.

Megan would never have known what the Students' Theatre was if she hadn't been told. Riina called the place a Palace of Culture. The building was a drab beige, shabby and peeling, and massive doors with cracked brown varnish tried to keep you out. "It was once a church. Now all manners of clubs, societies, classes gather here free of charges." Megan was amazed – free? But Nadya curled her lip. "If Communist authority give its precious approvement, only," she said. "And if no, then – it is forbidden."

Inside it was warm and bright, much glossier than the House of Culture where they had lunch. Wide stairs led up from the entrance hall, and students in jeans and loose sweaters dashed to and fro or gossiped in little groups. At the top of the stairs was a carpeted area hung with chandeliers and drapes. Megan felt excited. She took off her yellow hat and shook out her hair.

"Here," said Riina, running into the middle of the empty space, "if we are very, *very* good, and if they be *very* kind, the students may do drama with us school children."

Noises were coming from a door at the corner of the room. Nadya threw her coat over the banister, marched over to peer through and beckoned, finger to her lips. They crept across and stood at the door in the half darkness to watch what was going on.

This was the theatre, and they were at the back of the auditorium. A few young people sat scattered on the plush seats and, on stage, a line of girls with linked arms were practising their footwork. A cluster of boys sat on each side of the stage, dutifully silent during rehearsal.

Suddenly, deafening rock music was switched on. Then it was lowered to bearability, and the girls on stage started to sing and dance at full stretch.

"What's happening?" whispered Mish.

"The girls celebrate they adore to have sex with the boys," whispered Nadya.

Wow! What kind of a play was this? "Which one's Kostya?" Megan whispered to Riina.

"The right group, the left boy." Even in the dimness Megan could see her eyes glistening.

Right group, left boy. Kostya.

He was propped up on his arms, head flung right back and feet stuck straight out in front. It was an attitude that announced, "I'm one of the gang, but just a little set apart from it." He was slight, with longish light brown hair, and the legs of his jeans were paint-streaked and his trainers had knots in each lace.

Put your head up! Megan gave him orders from inside her head. *I want to see your face!* He did. He stared straight at where they were lurking.

Now she could see him properly. His jaw was narrow and his forehead broad, and even though his mouth was too small for the rest of his face, he seemed to be laughing without moving his lips at all.

No, he wasn't good-looking. His face was too much like an upturned triangle for that. Fanciable, though? Certainly. But she mustn't try to attract him. Riina wanted him, and Riina should have him. She turned her gaze decisively towards the dancing girls, and the swish of her hair brought back what Abi had said – "It's your hair, it'll drive Boris and Leonid wild."

Kostya went on staring at them. He nudged the boy beside him, a pale thin young man with tense-looking eyes and zig-zag eyebrows, but got no response. He kicked his legs up and down – lifted one shoulder and then the other – raised one eyebrow, then the other – leaned his head from side to side. All this directed towards the girls at the back.

An enraged bark from the middle of the auditorium, and a shaggy man with the build of an orang-utan leapt to his feet. The music and dancing stopped. The man stormed down the aisle, shouting and raising his fists at Kostya.

"That the director?" whispered Mish.

"That, yes, is Uncle Vanya," murmured Nadya. "Will he shoot Kostya upon this time, I ask, or send him to Siberia?"

Riina was trying to draw them away. "I do not like to watch. Poor boys, it is not fair with them," she explained, linking arms with Megan. "In this play there are so few times for men to sing and play, so many times for women. The men are bored."

Mish followed them to the top of the stairs and said, "Well, that's a change. Usually it's the men get all the best parts."

"But Yuri is not bored," Nadya said. "That is because Yuri possesses some thinking inside his head!"

"Yuri – is he the one next to Kostya?"

"Yes. Yuri becomes a philosopher," said Nadya. "He becomes in politics – "

"And he is being in love with you!" Riina teased Nadya.

"*Nyet!* That is gone, over!"

They could hear music again from the theatre. "Let's go back in," said Mish. "Can we sit and watch? And when there's a break, can you tell us what the play's all about?"

By the end of the rehearsal, Mish still hadn't had an answer. Lysistrata and her maidens had danced and sung and been yelled at by Uncle Vanya, the master of ceremonies had rehearsed his solo pieces (Riina whispered that this was the part Kostya coveted), the boys had practised fierce duels and tragic deaths. At ten o'clock Uncle Vanya packed them off with the verdict that they were, in

Nadya's translation, "a tribe of no-good bums".

This was the moment Riina and Nadya had been waiting for. They ushered Megan and Mish to the top of the stairs and sat down, leaning back casually and putting their leather boots up on spare seats as though they owned the place. They chatted and joked in Russian to the students as they drifted out of the theatre, but didn't introduce their British friends.

Megan and Mish glanced at each other, annoyed. How long was this going on? Would the parents be worried if they were back late?

Then Kostya appeared, and Yuri. They were deep in talk. Megan thought, "They're going to pass us by without even saying *Zdrastvuitye!*" Kostya reached the top step – and turned round and sauntered back to where the girls were sitting.

He bowed deeply, murmuring, *"Dobry vyecher!"* with exaggerated politeness. "Riina – Nadya. Delighted I am. This are your British friends?"

Nadya introduced them. Kostya bowed again and kissed each of their hands. Megan was embarrassed. How daft – he was behaving like something out of Noel Coward! Or did all Russians do this sort of thing? Yuri's eyes didn't leave Nadya for a second.

Kostya talked briefly to Riina in Russian and turned to Megan. "I am told by Riina much from you," he said. "You love our play-acting?"

Nervously she said, "Very much, thank you. I don't actually know the play – we haven't done any Greek drama yet."

Mish plunged in. "What on earth is the plot? Something to do with love and war – we couldn't make it out."

Kostya frowned exaggeratedly – or was he having difficulty composing his English? "Oh, it is in depth and fully significant. It touches one's heart, it gives torture to one's..." Lost for a word, he shouted something to Yuri who was on the far side of the room with Nadya.

"Soul!" Yuri called back.

"Torture to one's *soul*. It is when women would not – will not love these men because they fight too much war."

"I remember it!" Mish was devoid of embarrassment. "The women won't have sex with their husbands till they stop fighting!"

"Exact. You are exact." Kostya turned from Mish to Megan. "But you – you do not know this. You are – " and again he shouted something over to Yuri, who called something back in Russian and then pronounced, "in-no-cent".

"You are *innocent*," said Kostya. His gaze was fixed on Megan, she felt him take in her grey-green eyes, her fading freckles and her mass of hair. She'd got the remains of a pimple on her chin – would he notice? "Perhaps it is good – innocent, so to be. But it is ... nessary, *necessary*, to be learning, also. You will return, to theatre here, to learn."

"I'd like to do that, thanks very much." She must be formal, keep him at a distance. "I'm sorry, Riina, but shouldn't we go now? Your parents'll be getting anxious."

"Yes, yes," Riina said quickly, and shouted to

Nadya. Nadya, looking relieved, strode over. Mish asked, "Do the Metro trains run this late?"

"Metro trains, always we have Metro trains." Nadya dismissed the problem. "Only cars – travel – cafés – supermarkets – choosings – pleasure. Only these we lack. Come, let us go."

"But yesterday you come again." Kostya leaned forward. "No – *tomorrow*."

"Tomorrow we go to the Bolshoi," said Mish.

Yuri, in grave clear tones, said that tomorrow after rehearsal he planned to visit one of Moscow's best small experimental theatres. Might they, if they could tolerate omitting the lengthy ballet at the Bolshoi, join them there?

"I'm afraid not." Mish was firm. "Our teacher has been to great trouble arranging the Bolshoi visit. Perhaps we'll come back here later in the week."

"Yes, we will bring you to visit later, we will," said Riina.

As they said formal goodbyes, Kostya joked a little with Riina in Russian and Riina's eyes lit up as she joked back. She's like a lighthouse, Megan thought as she tucked her hair back into her hat. She beams out happiness and misery by turns. I mustn't hurt her.

She glanced back up from the bottom of the stairs. Kostya and Yuri were leaning over the banister. She could see Yuri's zig-zag eyebrows narrowing glumly, while Kostya's were raised in silent laughter. He caught her eye as she looked up, and raised one hand in a kind of salute.

* * *

Nadya and Riina sat on one side of the train chatting in Russian, and Megan sat with Mish on the other side chatting in English. Mish described another Greek play she once saw, went on to Chekhov's *Uncle Vanya* and ended up with *Waiting for Godot*. Was she trying to stop Megan drifting into a romantic fantasy about Kostya?

She tried to guess what Nadya and Riina were talking about. Sometimes Nadya seemed to be trying to comfort Riina, though she couldn't be sure.

When they got off, Riina and Nadya started to argue. Nadya gestured angrily as they went up the steps, and Riina tried to calm her down. Out in the sharp night air Mish asked, "What's wrong? D'you think we're out too late or something?"

"Nadya feels it is necessary to take a taxi now. I feel no."

"A taxi? We can walk – it's not far."

Nadya rattled off some Russian to Riina. Riina said carefully, "It is the question of crime. Nadya feels there is great crime, men stop and take from us. But I say no, it is nothing, it is only talk."

Megan felt a flutter of fear. Was Moscow like London for street crime? Or even New York? "You mean there's mugging? People hitting you over the head, grabbing your money?"

"Yes, yes!" cried Nadya.

"No, it is nothing, truly!" insisted Riina. "You do not know, Nadya – you have not seen what London is – I have seen it on TV – "

Mish was amazed. "You see British TV *here*?"

"Not here, no," said Riina excitedly. "In Tallinn, where I live. It is so near to Finland, sixty kilometres across the sea, we get TV of England, TV of United States – films, many films. So many crimes, so much killings there! In Tallinn, in Moscow even, it is not here so criminal. Do not believe Nadya."

Nadya was furious. "Taxi, money, we have money." Riina admitted their parents had given them money for a taxi just in case.

"That settles it," decided Mish. "Better be safe than sorry. Let's find a taxi. OK, Megan?"

"OK," said Megan. But she was not OK. She was shaking inside. Crime – anger – people rattling off in a language she didn't understand –

A battered-looking taxi was parked near by. Nadya leaned down to speak to the driver. Megan's heart pounded. Russian-scale emotions were mounting. Nadya took a pace back and the driver shoved out his irate face – lined as Oleg's and with three days' growth of beard – to shout at her. Worse, he kept gesturing towards Megan and Mish as though the row were about them.

Nadya had rapid words with Riina. They nodded, and Nadya tugged open the back door. "All in," she ordered. Megan could see springs sticking up from the upholstery of the back seat.

Then the driver barked out something else. Nadya, who was getting in first, backed sharply out again. "*Nyet, nyet!*" She slammed the door and marched back towards the Metro station. The others ran after her.

Megan grabbed Riina's sleeve. "What happened?"

"It is nothing." Riina's tone suddenly switched.

79

She sounded resigned, as if these incidents happened every day. "He was willing only if we gave currency."

"Currency?"

"Hard currency – dollars, pounds. He sees you and Mish are English. He asks pounds. We say no, rude, you are visitors, he is rude. That is all."

Telephones, taxis, money – nothing worked here! You couldn't take anything for granted. Exciting it might be, one minute, but it was terrifying the next.

"Now we walk," said Riina. "We walk," repeated Nadya, gloomily. "Michelle?" Mish shrugged her shoulders at Megan, and the two pairs went off in opposite directions.

Riina and Megan walked in silence till they were near home. Then Riina started to talk stiffly about the theatre. Would she mention Kostya? If so, what was Megan to say – what a nice guy he was, or that she'd hated him on sight?

She was saved from having to say either. Riina stopped outside the lift, turned and spoke intensely. "You will understand," she said, "that it is most secret I wish Kostya to prefer me. My parents, they wish only for me to marry a Estonian boy. In four months we return to Tallinn and join with our compatriots to proclaim independence for our country. My parents could not tolerate for me to love with a Russian boy. Me too! I wish I will marry a Estonian boy!"

"But you can have a nice time with Kostya, can't you, while you're in Moscow? You don't have to get married and settle down just yet."

"Of course. I will go to the Institute and make my career with translating, I will travel, maybe even to England. But in Soviet Union, you know, all women pursue the career in addition to the home and the baby."

"Yes, but – marry! I don't want to get married for years – maybe ever!"

"Ever? Megan! You will fall into love, you will marry!"

"Maybe, maybe not. I could just move in and live with a bloke. We might get married if I got pregnant, I suppose."

"Megan! You love, you marry, then you have a baby!"

Megan's stomach lurched. Had she rushed in with two left feet? Change the subject, quick. "Yes, well… Probably things are different with us. Look, Riina, I know you feel strongly about Estonia. But I live in Wales, you know. Don't go on about 'England' as though that's all there is. My friend Dafydd would go mad if he heard you."

"He? This boy, he is your special friend?"

Yes, he is my special friend, thought Megan. And when I go on with my letter to him, what am I going to write about Kostya?

"Wales," Riina was saying. "I am so sorry, Megan. Oleg Stepanovich said especially we must remember Wales. We learnt how to say some words in your language – "

"Not *my* language – I'm English actually, but my parents wanted to live in Wales for Kate's health, not that it's done her any good – then I was

81

born and they called me Megan to make themselves feel more at home. I quarrel with Dafydd over Welsh, I think they make too much of a song and dance about it actually…"

Riina grabbed her elbow to stop the flow. "Listen to my clever Welsh words. *Bore da – Eisteddfod – un, dau, tri –* "

"Riina! You even got the 'dd' right! Listen, I'll teach you the song we were belting out this morning. *Pan fo'r storm – yn ei grym – paid ac ofni dim…* And don't – be afraid – of the dark…"

"Ssssssh!" whispered Riina with a giggle. "They will all awake! But they tell us it is a footballing song – how is that?"

"It's this team, Liverpool, it's their signature tune. Sorry –" Megan's mind suddenly disintegrated like soggy paper. "It's no good, I'm too tired, I can't explain. Can I just fall into bed?"

CHAPTER FIVE

Carelessly turned-up coat collars, lipsticked mouths, long curling eyelashes, a coloured neckscarf. Autumn chic of the Arbat.

Anatoli Rybakov, *Children of the Arbat*

Day three was a strange, empty sort of day. When they gathered at the Salyut Hotel, Ellen announced coldly that Oleg was ill this morning, but they would continue with their timetable as planned. Megan was longing to tell everyone about the Students' Theatre, but no one asked. Maybe everyone was dazed by Moscow, the language problems and enforced friendships. She and Riina were the only two who seemed relaxed together. Even Mish and Nadya were silent after last night's row.

Sylvia took them inside the Kremlin, and everyone was surprised to find it was a park rather than a fortress. The domes of numerous cathedrals glimmered gently against a gun-metal sky. When they went inside a cathedral for ten minutes, Megan found herself impressed by the intricacy of the ancient painted icons, and was glad she was near Olwen and could say so.

Outside again, Olwen said she was puzzled. Where were all the Super-Comrades? This couldn't be the place where government went on?

"No, no," said Sylvia, "the government buildings are over there. And here I wish to indicate the point where Napoleon came marching after the Battle of Borodino – but our courage and our winter weather sent him home, as they did more recently Hitler also."

Back in Red Square they were pestered by gangs of kids trying to exchange cheap Lenin badges for bubblegum. When Tom sent them off with a flea in their ear, Ellen was angry. Didn't he realize even food was rationed here, and luxuries like bubblegum far beyond any kid's pocket money?

The afternoon drama workshops lacked sparkle. Ellen was listless, though she led them through a mime of "Family Crisis, East and West" which they managed to get some laughs out of. Megan was in a group with Abi's partner, Nina, who Abi had nicknamed "The Walking Tank". Nina played a fat *babushka*, with Spock as a rebellious teenager and Megan as a wailing baby. While she was acting, Nina began to unbend. She went into livid shock-horror at the sight of the three earrings in Spock's earlobes and mimed a tearful "Never darken my doors again". Megan had a great time acting the baby. She grabbed hold of one of Nina's solid legs at a crucial moment, and while Nina was sobbing with anger she sneaked off to grab an imaginary glass of vodka and down it in one.

As the workshop ended and they split up to go off to their respective flats, Megan had a quiet word with Mish. They agreed they'd rather go to

Yuri's theatre than to the Bolshoi, but no, tonight they ought to stay with the gang.

She managed to survive the ballet, which she'd despised as namby-pamby tutu-twirling when she had seen it on TV. She sat beside Abi, who adored it, and passed her tissues while the dying swan danced herself to death. She even sniffed a bit herself.

Coming out with the crowds from the Bolshoi theatre, she glanced round the milling masses in case Kostya and Yuri might appear. But they didn't. Riina seemed alert too, but neither of them confessed it. Back they went to the flat for more bread and cheese and sweet cakes with Mr and Mrs Tormis. The talk was of whether Riina would go to the University of Tartu when they got home. Home! They spoke as if they were exiles here in Moscow.

Riina said that before they went to bed she must make a note of the English vocabulary she'd learnt that day, while Megan must feel free to write to her favourite Welsh boy. So Megan plumped up the pillows on her sofa-bed and settled herself with pen in hand.

But what should she say to Dafydd? She started describing the icons, but screwed it up – he wouldn't be interested in icons. Or would he? He was doing GCSE Art, wasn't he? She realized there was a lot she still didn't know about Dafydd.

Words formed in her mind. "The real event was going to the Students' Theatre – meeting Kostya and Yuri – Yuri's obviously wild about Nadya, and Kostya..." No, she'd leave it. She'd write about

85

Kostya if they went back to the dress rehearsal or the performance.

She started scribbling a postcard to Mum and Dad and Kate. "Tomorrow we're off to visit Lenin in his Mausoleum..." She and Riina said their formal goodnights and she snuggled down. It took her a long time to get to sleep, and when she finally drifted off she was floating into a fantasy about Kostya whisking her to Gorky Park for a secret embrace.

By the morning she'd forgotten her fantasies and was determined to consider the Soviet Union and its complexities with all due seriousness.

Lenin's embalmed corpse was almost transparent, the colour of ivory tinged with steel. His suit was dark grey, his beard and eyebrows palest grey. His catafalque was protected by glass – bullet-proof, in case someone shot him? – and he looked heartless as well as bloodless, not caring a jot about the hushed queue of reverential people tiptoeing endlessly by. Megan yearned for him to sit bolt upright and say, "Look, I'm Lenin, and I'm dead. I've been dead sixty-five years. If I were a waxwork from Madame Tussaud's you wouldn't know any difference. So how about giving me a decent burial at long last?"

She was sure someone would snort with laughter before they were out of the building. But nobody did. They filed, in pairs, in total silence. Round the catafalque – you weren't allowed to stop for a moment – down the carpeted steps, round the marbled corner, up the steps again and out into the cold. Then there was more enforced queuing, enforced reverence. You had to trudge along the Kremlin Wall to admire the plaques commemorating Soviet heroes, including the dreaded Stalin. Out at last into the wide open cobbled spaces of Red Square: only then could you relax, unbutton your coat, breathe easily again.

Lenin. Why was everyone caught up in reverence for this man? His portrait was everywhere, hanging beside hammer-and-sickle flags and posters of Gorbachev with his birthmark painted out. Lenin seemed more than a leader, more even than a hero – like a god. What had happened to religion?

And what was wrong with Oleg yesterday? He was back again this morning, looking subdued. Would he be in charge of the workshops this afternoon? Riina said that this evening they were going to the Arbat.

"Who or what's the Arbat?" she asked Abi as they walked back to the coach.

"Dunno. Hey, have you heard there's a party over at our place tomorrow? What d'you reckon a party of Nina's'll be like?"

"Lectures on Marxist Leninism, most likely," said Tom, walking alongside. "Washed down with glasses of weak tea."

Lunch was at the same House of Culture, the same spread of bread, cheese and coleslaw. No fresh salad or fruit, no variation on processed cheese slices. Megan sat with Mish, Tom and Meredydd, and noticed that most tables were Moscow-only or Brits-only.

"What's your food like?" Tom asked, his voice low. "I'm sure my lot keep hens in the lift-shaft – we've had chicken every single meal!"

"Mine are very kind and all that," said Meredydd, "but they serve me food on a plate in the living room and won't let me near the kitchen. My parents told me to be sure and help with the washing up."

"But they're so generous!" said Mish. "You only have to say 'Isn't that pretty' and they shove it in your hand – 'For you, for you'. Nadya gave me her headscarf this morning."

"Seriozha's determined I'll have his chess set," said Meredydd. "Great heavy stuff it is, ivory or something – I'll never get it in my suitcase!"

"You know something I've noticed?" Mish said to Megan, as Tom and Meredydd lapsed into Welsh.

"What?"

"No seagulls."

"Roast, for lunch, like pigeon pie?"

Mish nudged the coleslaw off Megan's fork. "Flying around, dafto. Well, have you seen one? No sea – no seagulls."

Megan considered. "Not a single." When you came to think of it, seagulls were everywhere back home. Even driving down the M6 you'd hear their cry as flocks of them swooped on a newly ploughed field. "Only those monstrous things, jackdaws, and a couple of grubby sparrows if you're lucky."

They went by trolley-bus back to the drama studio for the workshop, crowding on like a gang of fans on their way to a match. ("No such luck," grumbled Spock in one of his rare utterances. "World Cup Qualifier's been transferred to the Crimea. Where on earth's that?") None of the Brits knew how to pay their fare. Then Vitya called, "Come, Welskis, have your five kopeks!" and they realized that everyone was passing five-kopek pieces up to the front of the bus.

At the studio, Ellen stood in the shadows and left the afternoon entirely to Oleg. Oleg, yesterday's illness unexplained, was in a severe mood. His clothes were a size too big for him and his shoulders hunched and tense.

"A ring. On chairs. Pentre Moscow alternate. Neat, I ask you." Then – "Levan!" A snapped instruction, and Levan moved his chair to complete the smooth circle.

Oleg was the last to sit down. He put his finger to his lips: *Mime.* Then he took a cigarette packet out of his pocket, put it to his unkempt hair and used it as a comb. His eyes panned the circle: *Understood?* Understood.

He handed the cigarette packet to Jim, who polished his shoes and handed it to Nina. Nina smiled as she took it from him, held it for a moment, then put it to her mouth and played it like a harmonica. Abi shook it and dabbed some perfume behind her ears. Seriozha threw it like a hand grenade and ran for cover. Meredydd stood fiddling with his trouser belt, sat down and pulled imaginary paper from the packet to wipe his bum. Everyone laughed except Oleg, who frowned and nodded for the packet to be passed on. When

Megan's turn came, she was struck by the reek of tobacco and tore it into imaginary shreds to light like a fire.

Then Oleg carried his chair into the centre. He pointed to Nadya. "Come, sit. This way." Nadya sat according to instruction, backwards in the chair and clutching it for comfort, head down and hair covering her face, a picture of grief.

"Come," ordered Oleg. "Any, when your spirit tells you. Cheer her."

Silence. No movement. Who would be first? Megan was nervous. What if she couldn't think what to do? If Oleg snapped at her?

Riina stood and walked thoughtfully over. Megan felt her absorption in the task, yet she was reacting to every vibration from Oleg. Riina put a hand tentatively towards Nadya's hair and touched it in a single gentle stroke. Nadya jerked her head: *Get off.* Riina, rejected, returned to her seat.

Silence. No movement. No one wanted to take the risk.

Oleg pointed a finger round. It stopped at Olwen.

Olwen paused, then walked confidently, carrying her chair. She sat down like a teacher, gestured to Nadya about the interesting things she was missing and tried to lift her chin. No go. Nadya's chin stuck fiercely down on her chest.

Oleg lifted his finger once again. *Let it not point at me*, Megan prayed. The bony finger travelled the circle and ended up pointing at Jim.

Jim looked terrified. Everyone knew he couldn't

act. He was the keenest of them all, but on stage his body was gawky and his lines were stiff. Ellen must have chosen him for reliability, not talent. It flashed across Megan's mind: *Jim doesn't know how to act, because he's acting all the time.* It was true. Jim never relaxed, he was always wondering what his lines were.

He must have decided that macho was the appropriate style. He marched up to Nadya, put his hands on both sides of her chair and tugged it out from underneath her. She fell, stood up in a flash and grabbed the chair again. Startled, Jim lost both the chair and his footing and went smack! on his back on to the floor. Nadya lifted the chair in attack.

Nadya certainly could act. The chair hadn't actually touched Jim, but Megan was on her feet before she knew it to protect him. She ran forward – so did several others —

But before anyone else could get to him, Nina the Walking Tank had moved like lightning to the scene. She seized Nadya from behind and held her in an iron grip. Nadya struggled, but dropped the chair. Jim got shakily to his feet, rubbing his back in pain.

Megan expected the exercise to stop now – then everyone would have relaxed and laughter broken out. Ellen had emerged from the shadows and was waiting behind Megan to suggest the next task.

But Oleg, standing behind Nina who still had Nadya in her hold, put his hand up. "Continue!" His eyes compelled them. Not Levan, not Ellen dared say, "Come off it, Oleg – the game's over."

91

All except the central tableau moved away and sat down.

Jim stood rubbing his hurt back. He was close to tears. You can't just let him stand there, Megan thought – if Jim wept in public he'd die of shame! Nina wasn't looking at him. She was grimly tightening her grip on Nadya, who struggled to get free.

It was Vitya who saw what had to be done. He strode over to the little group, pointed a gun at Nina's head and jerked it back and forth between the two girls. Nina glared, but was forced to release Nadya. Nadya stormed off across the room, kicking over Vitya's chair as she went. Vitya put his imaginary gun in its holster, picked up the original chair and ambled away.

Nina and Jim were left staring at each other. She went over and took his hand. Megan realized she'd never seen Jim hold hands with anyone before. Oleg said nothing, but watched Nina leading Jim gently back to his place.

"Arbat is for shopping and for culture," Riina told her. They were setting off to meet the others at the Metro. "There are many artists with their paintings, musicians, shops for books, gifts and so on and so forth."

Megan was beginning to get streetwise. "What do we buy them with? Roubles or pounds sterling?"

"One or the other," replied Riina. "But – " screwing up her nose – "for many, many roubles, or few, few pounds."

"Riina – " began Megan, a lump rising in her throat, "when will we be going back to the Students' Theatre? Ellen and Oleg have arranged such a heavy programme..."

"We will. We must. The chief rehearsal of their play – "

"Dress rehearsal?"

"Is tomorrow. Then the day for the Revolution anniversary, the parade, and at night the fireworks. Then, the night next – performance."

"We must go! We can't miss that!"

"So I think also. And I ... I told to Kostya the programme of our group. I thinked – I thought, he would wish to see me on account I have enticing friends."

"I'm sure he likes you, Riina. Don't get any ideas about me fancying him. Dafydd's my bloke, I don't want anyone else."

"But I do not wish him! I must not love a Russian boy!"

"Moscow's a great place, though. Maybe you could stay on?"

"No! Not permitted, anyhow."

"Oh?" She didn't understand. "Maybe you'll find Tallinn boring when you get back."

"Boring, my home? Never. Moscow is not great, Megan. Moscow is oppression. You must know, Stalin took many of our people in cattle wagons – like Jewish people into Auschwitz – to Siberian wasteland, to work, to die..."

They were nearly at the Metro and Megan expected Riina to change the subject abruptly. But no: "Then Stalin, he sends thousands of Russian

93

people to live in our Estonia, to crush us, take our earth and jobs…"

"But it's the Soviet Union now, surely?" asked Megan as they went to stand beside Mish and Nadya. "You're all one, aren't you?" She caught sight of Mr Haigh's giraffe-like face looking amazed at their earnest politics.

"No! The Estonian flag will be raised in Tallin! Soon, soon!"

Olwen took over. "What do you think's going to happen in the Baltic States, Riina?" Megan was half annoyed, half relieved. Sometimes her head began to hurt. Riina and Estonia was as bad as Dafydd with his Welsh Nationalism.

The sun had struggled to emerge at the end of the afternoon. They came up from Arbatskaya station to see it glowing over the elegant old buildings, mellowing their shabbiness. The street in front of them was pedestrians-only, and cobbled.

"You must buy here paintings for your mother the artist," said Riina as they put up their collars against the cold. "Presents too for your poor Kate. Must she be all day in her bed?"

Abi butted in. "Kate in her bed? What on earth d'you mean? I live next door to the Shipways — "

"No," interrupted Megan. "It's not that bad, it's only asthma."

"And in what galleries does your mother exhibit her artistry?"

Abi opened her mouth again and Megan blustered something about "local artist only". Oh God, she shouldn't have tried to impress Riina in her letter. Next minute she'd be asking if her father was in the Olympics!

Ellen and Oleg called them to order. "Listen, everyone. Tie! I said listen!"

"Young people, your attention." Oleg made some laughing comment to Ellen in Russian as the group shuffled into silence. His face relaxed into laughter-lines instead of grooves. "Enjoy our Arbat! Here you will see the pavement painters packing their bags as the light fades. Soon come the musicians, the sweet strings and the heavy rock. But in the Arbat we must beware the hooligans. Perhaps we are lucky, perhaps tonight there will be none."

"You can go off on your own now," said Ellen. "In pairs, please, no one alone, preferably fours. We'll meet here again at – what time, Oleg?"

"How long a time do we need, Yelyena? Perhaps, nine o'clock?"

Megan and Riina got into a group with Mish and Nadya, then Olwen and Masha joined them and Abi came too. Nina joined Jim and Dima and went off towards the big book shop in Kalinin Prospekt.

Oleg was right, the street artists were packing up their easels. A little farther along a couple of student artists showed their wares: sets of ten Russian dolls in diminishing sizes which, instead of gaudy flowers and patterns, were painted with icons almost as vivid and delicate as the ones in the Kremlin Cathedrals. *Skolka stoyeet?* asked Olwen. "One thousand five hundred roubles," answered the girl.

Megan gasped. "A hundred and fifty pounds!"

"Eight months of wages for my mother, almost," said Nadya. "For dolls!"

A group of lads, looking almost Western in their scruffiness, were unpacking saxophones, guitars and a double bass. "Rock! I know them!" cried Nadya and ran towards them.

"Our Nadya," commented Riina. "Rock, the West. It is all she lives for."

"D'you think she'll get there?" asked Mish.

"Who can tell. Many, many wish to go. Kostya also – " she turned to Megan as the others' attention was drawn to the rock band starting to play. "He also wishes to be there, the West. Let us walk on, alone." She ran over to have a word with Nadya, then came back to Megan and took her arm. "To Kostya, I said we might be a little way –" and she pointed ahead.

"You arranged to meet him?"

"Not meet. Just maybe … knock into, you say?"

They wandered along, gazing into shops full of art books, pressing their noses against the windows of expensive restaurants. "But soon," she said, "there is a place for us…"

"'Somewhere a place for us…'" Megan started to sing. "D'you know it? *West Side Story* – I'm Anita – we're going to perform bits of it."

"A Georgian centre, we can have drinks there, no alcohol, it is good for young people. I told to Kostya."

As Riina said his name, Megan saw him among the crowds in the distance. Was it him? Yes. He was on his own. He had a tennis-player's hairband round his head and he was sauntering along, pausing every so often to kick a small stone from between the cobbles.

"I told that is where we might be. Tell me, Megan, tell me about your Daf – what is his name?"

"Dafydd. He's mad about music, like Nadya, and about his country, like you…"

Riina tightened her grip on Megan's arm. She'd seen Kostya too. They both stopped, as if not wanting to approach him.

He had seen them. His face lightened, and he strode over and made his small bow. "Riina – " (Megan was sure he wouldn't remember her name) – "Megan." He pronounced it "Maygann". "I – late for rehearsal. No matter. It is good to see."

Riina nodded silently. Megan said, "Nice to see you, Kostya."

"I thought you would not find," said Riina.

"A lemon tree, my dear Watson."

Megan's jaw dropped. "A *what* my dear Watson?"

"Alementree," said Kostya, puzzled. "That is incorrect? We have the Sherlock Holmes on all the cinema-films."

"Oh, *elementary*!" Megan laughed. "'Elementary, my dear Watson'! I thought you said 'A lemon tree' – lemon, like in oranges and lemons!"

Riina didn't laugh. "Lemon – *limon*," she explained to Kostya quietly.

Now Kostya laughed with Megan. Riina was

excluded. She glanced sharply behind her and said to Megan, "There come the others near. I join them. We will meet, nine o'clock, Arbatskaya Metro." She turned to walk away.

"But – Riina! You want…" Megan called after her. "We were told, pairs only!" Anxiously she said to Kostya, "Our teacher said we were not to be alone." Riina didn't turn back.

"Alone? You be with me," said Kostya, taking her arm and walking firmly back the way he had come. "Nine of the clock. We have near one hour."

He walked at a cracking pace far down Arbat Street. Where were they going? Megan was breathless from trying to keep up with him, and because his arm was linked through hers.

"Georgian," he said as he led her up the steps of a building. Ah! The Georgian Centre Riina had mentioned. She relaxed a little. "Here is a gentle place. Happy for children, old women, lovers. No vodka, no wine, no men who – " and he fell about like a drunkard. Past showcases of Georgian art, down a spiral staircase, and she found they were in a lushly decorated basement café. Kostya gestured her to a small round table in a corner while he fetched glasses of fizzy fruit juice. "Special to Georgian region, most tasty," he said.

She sat on an upholstered velvet chair, surrounded by abstract art collages and embroideries, and waited for him. What was going to happen now? Would she find her way back to the others? She was hot and sweaty from the walk, and her heart was beating up in her throat. She'd keep her hair tucked up in her yellow felt hat – she must not, *must* not drive Kostya wild. How stupid, Abi was stupid – but –

He came and sat down with the drinks and said, "Sorry, sorry if you are alarm, Maygann. I find interest in you. Riina is kind girl, she knows I find interest in England."

"But what about your rehearsal?"

"The scenes do not possess me tonight. Now. Tell me all of England."

"But I don't live in England!" She forgot her sweat and her heartbeat: she was off and away. In between sips of fizzy fruit juice she told him about Wales, Pentre, the Clwyd hills, the beaches at Rhyl and Llandudno, about Chester and Dad's school – "I told Riina he was an athlete, you know, like in the Olympics, but he isn't at all, he just supervises school football" – and her mother's watercolours of Snowdonia, about Kate and Dafydd and the Welsh language and Pentre's production of *West Side Story* and Bryn Corach's of *Carousel*. He didn't interrupt. His eyes fixed themselves on hers, and he listened to every word.

His eyes were mottled grey, specked with black. She found the specks so fascinating that sometimes she had to lower her own eyes and speak to the glass on the table. He was the best listener she'd ever met.

Maybe that was because he didn't understand a word? "I'm sorry – I'm talking too much, too fast, I'm rabbiting on..."

"Rabbit – why is rabbit? It is wonderful, Maygann. I understand not all, but much. All this years I learn English, and never do I know if it means true, if it is real. Now I know, it is real! You are wonderful."

"I'm not, really. Now you must tell me about you, your home and family. I'm sorry, I don't have any Russian at all. Your English is marvellous, honestly. Hey, what about the time?"

"It is early, early."

"Eight forty-eight! It'll take quarter of an hour to get back to the Metro!"

"Eight, nine minutes only. No worry, we will arrive."

He tossed down the rest of his juice as he stood up. Then he took her arm and they half walked, half ran up the spiral staircase and out, back along the cobbled Arbat.

There was no time or breath to talk any more. Clocks were striking nine just as they caught sight of the group. Riina was standing apart from the rest, and when she saw the two of them she hurried forward.

Megan was so breathless she couldn't speak to Kostya. He let go of her arm, said, "Rehearsal! Tomorrow! Be there, both two!" Then he ran off.

CHAPTER SIX

"We have drunk to friendship and to love: these are great and timeless things," said Rubin.

Solzhenitzin, *The First Circle*

She woke. A pearly light was beginning to appear at the bedroom window, just enough to write by. She'd slept well and dreamlessly, and her head was clear. Dafydd. She'd go on with her letter, and she'd tell him about Kostya.

Riina had chatted with exaggerated brightness all the way home. But her English went suddenly haywire: "See the light brights for this o'clock of our Revolution!" Abi had tried to sit near them on the Metro, but Ruskies and Welskies fell into the seats between them so she was forced into the company of her parents and the Walking Tank.

Megan composed a witty sentence. "The USSR is divided into two sorts of people – the dead ones and the live ones. The dead ones are Lenin, Stalin, Nina and Abi's mum (if only she'd apply for political asylum). The live ones are Oleg (yes, he's alive and dynamic even tho' he's so strange and sort of oppressed-looking) & Vitya & Nadya & Riina & Kostya & I think Yuri too. Yuri's a student at the theatre – we've only met him once but R.

says he's a dissident politico. Kostya's another, he met us yesterday in the Arbat (bit like Covent Garden) and we went to a Georgian caff" (she congratulated herself on the truth of her wording) "and I told him all about Pentre Corach, *Carousel*, you, etc." What an audience he'd been. His speckled eyes hadn't glazed over once – he hadn't interrupted with a single story about his own brilliant career. "Hey, Daf, d'you think Ellen really was heading for Big Stuff with old Griff? She seems to have this on-off tensed-up thing with Crumpleface Oleg. I don't reckon it's..."

Riina stirred and turned over towards Megan's sofa-bed. Her eyelids fluttered. Then she turned back again. Was she avoiding conversation – hurt that Kostya had taken Megan away? But she'd engineered it!

Bang! The front door: Mr Tormis off to work. Sounds of Mrs Tormis preparing breakfast came from the kitchen. Megan felt guilty. They'd come back too late to say goodnight to Riina's parents two evenings out of four. She decided to leave her letter, slip on her jeans and go to the kitchen to chat.

Bathroom first. She crept across the hall. So many books! The Tormises must be intellectuals – the types Stalin hated. Might her grandparents have been carted off to Siberia like cattle? She opened the bathroom door. Kostya the cat uncurled from his cushion and glided over to rub himself against her. "Hello, Kostya," she whispered. "Sleep well? I did, like a log." Where did Kostya sleep? Did he live with his parents, on his own, in a student hostel – where?

"Megan!" Mrs Tormis was peeling a bowl of beetroot, her hands stained purple. "You sleep good?"

"Marvellously, thanks. Can I do anything to help?"

"*Nyet* – guest persons not work, please."

Megan stood awkwardly. She wanted to make conversation but didn't know how.

"Apologies, Megan, I speak not you in Welsh. Riina say Wales people love the Welsh, not the speaking English."

"No – I hardly speak Welsh. Lots of people do, but — "

"Not speak? But why? We speak the Estonian!"

"Please, can you tell me a bit about Estonia? Oh – you've got a flag!" A red flag with a wide blue wavy stripe was pinned to the kitchen curtain.

"I show." Mrs Tormis wiped her hands on a damp cloth and went to pull the curtain. "Blue – for ocean. Estonia has much ocean, Baltic, with –" she gestured with her stained hand. "Waves," prompted Megan.

"We pull curtain – so." She drew the curtain so that most of the flag unfurled. "But not ... so." She drew it farther, revealing the Soviet hammer and sickle in the corner. "We not like to see!" – and she pulled back the curtain to hide the Soviet symbol again.

"In Wales we have the dragon," said Megan.

"Dra...?"

"Animal – not real – breathes fire – " Megan puffed and made flames with her hands.

"Ah! *Drakon!*"

103

They both laughed, then looked up. Riina appeared in the doorway, hair dishevelled, still in her nightdress. "Megan. Good day," she said glumly. "This morning we visit Exhibition of Soviet Economic Achievements."

"Well, that sounds a bundle of fun," answered Megan, trying to break through the cloud. "What do we get to see? Lumps of steel, bags of coal?"

"Is exhibited showcases of pretty costumes and artefacts from all republics including Estonia. I went many times."

"And were bored out of your tiny mind."

Mrs Tormis stopped chopping beetroot. "Is Museum of Space there. Gagarin, Sputnik, yes? Is good, thrills for young persons. Riina – " And in what must be Estonian, for Megan now recognized the throatiness of Russian, she sent Riina off to get dressed.

Abi grabbed Megan as soon as they got to the Salyut Hotel, and started to quiz her about Kostya. "You went off on your tod with that lad! Spill, or I'll tell my mum!"

"No, he just wanted to know about Western stuff – theatre, rock."

"But Riina left you to it!"

"She's fed up with him, that's why. He keeps trailing round after her wherever she goes." That's clever, she thought. It'll save me having to explain if Kostya turns up again. I seem to be lying quite a lot these days.

Behind them, Nina was boasting over the aisle to Mr and Mrs Garth Jones about her video recorder and the films they'd be watching at her party. "Poser," murmured Abi. "Hey, guess what? Jim came to our place yesterday." "Jim did?" "Nina invited him round for her mother to give his poor back a herbal rub! Noticed Mish and Nadya, by the way?"

Nadya and Mish had swapped clothes. They were up at the front of the coach just now, talking to Ellen – Nadya with Mish's jeans hanging baggily round her hips and a split knee revealing a portion of slim thigh, Mish with her solid bum squeezed into Nadya's snow-washed outfit.

Their Intourist bus was stopping. "To our left," intoned Sylvia as if for the thousandth time, "you see a monument to the glories of Soviet space exploration. You will remember Yuri Gagarin, the first spaceman, a Soviet citizen. In the museum are given many tributes to our space hero, and many hundred wonderful displays."

Two hours later, those who'd tried to concentrate were suffering from mental indigestion, and those who hadn't, from terminal boredom.

"God, I'm dying for a fag," moaned Abi. "Mum's spying on me all the time! Why do we have to trail round these places? Why can't we go to this school of theirs, help them mug up on their precious English?"

"Schools are closed for Revolution week, thickhead," said Megan. "1917 and All That. Parade tomorrow, fireworks in the evening, remember?"

Then back to the House of Culture for the same old lunch. Today the apartheid between Brits and

Muscovites was even more marked. Megan was sitting with Tie, Spock and Abi.

Tie picked up a bowl of greasy coleslaw and aimed it across the table. "Anyone for custard pie?" Abi grabbed it out of his hand. "But that's all it's fit for," protested Tie. "And look at this!" He seized a triangle of flabby cheese, held it over his head and started declaiming in Oleg's accent, "See, the most latest fashion in our headscarves!"

Spock grabbed the cheese out of Tie's hand and put it against his chin – a beard. He handed it to Megan. Megan was tempted to use it as toilet paper, but felt Ellen's eye across the room. She chopped the corners off to make a rectangle and handed it to Abi – "One rouble change, madam."

"No, honestly," Abi burst out, "it's all so *shabby*! The buildings have great chunks falling off, the flats are like rabbit hutches – even Nina's, and Olwen says Nina's a regular party apparatchik." Megan stopped munching her salami in mid-chew. Things were looking up if Abi was getting the lingo. "She says she's the only one with a washing machine! The roads are full of potholes, the loos smell like cess-pits – then they drag you off to some fancy exhibition to show what a brilliant country they've got!"

"Can't get out either," grunted Spock.

"What?" said Tie. "No – no currency, no travel. I tell a lie – I heard Nina showing off about some holiday in Bulgaria."

They all laughed. Where was Bulgaria, anyway? "And GUM – what did you make of GUM?" asked Abi.

"Then there's Chernobyl," said Tie. "Llyr's sheep are still unsaleable! After how many years?"

"Have you seen a Soviet hair-drier? Nina's is a sort of metal box, with a grid on the side that the air's supposed to come out of. I asked if I could borrow it, but she couldn't get it to work. So she tried to puff my hair with her own breath! A genuine blow dry!"

"Er-hum – " Megan gestured surreptitiously towards Riina sitting at the next table with Masha, Sonya and Nadya.

Abi glanced round. "It's OK," she said. "He can't hear right across the room." He? Megan realized she meant Oleg. "Isn't it amazing," Abi went on in an affected tone, "how they can get hold of carnations even in this weather?"

Off to the studio theatre for workshops. Riina joined up with Megan again. Megan was afraid she'd ask her about Abi's lunchtime gripes, but clearly Riina's mind was on other things. In a private moment while brushing their hair in the Ladies, she said casually, "Kostya favours you a little, I think?"

"No, he's just hooked on the West, I'm certain of it. He won't cough up anything about his own life, though, will he?"

"Hooked – cough? Where is my notebook to write these?"

"Riina, are we going to get to the dress rehearsal tonight?"

"I think it is not possible. Nina's party is compulsory." They grinned at each other and groaned. "But the performance –" Riina added, "– we go."

* * *

107

Ellen was in charge of the workshops today. "Groups of three!" she called. Pairs ran round chasing a third, and (Mer having retired to bed with a cold) Jim and Nina were left out on their own. "Now four! Five!" Mr and Mrs Garth Jones, who'd had enough of sightseeing, joined in so they could make up five lots of five.

In their groups of five, Ellen asked them to create sculptures: of a space capsule, of a *balalaika*, then of *perestroika*. "*Perestroika*? What kind of a sculpture can you make of that?" Megan was with Masha, Mike, Annest and Levan, but she found herself airing possibilities with Annest in English while the other three were in a separate huddle doing the same in Russian. "This is no good," she said. "What d'you lot think? We've decided it should be something to do with sweetness and light – harmony."

"Most interesting," said Levan drily. "We favoured the interpretation that *perestroika* is not harmony, but chaos."

For their next exercise Ellen gave them each the name of a country and told them to create the map of Europe. Tie thought Yugoslavia was one of the Baltic States and Abi put Luxembourg south of Italy, but eventually they got themselves arranged.

"I am Berlin," said Oleg, pushing his way to the centre. "I am the capital of the whole of Germany." He clutched on to Llyr, who was supposed to be East Germany. "Oh!" cried Oleg. "I cannot be in both the Germanys at one time! I am breaking in pieces! Yelyena, come to be my second half!"

Much giggling followed, and falling about. This was one of Ellen and Oleg's better days.

When they were back in a circle, Ellen told the groups to separate and rehearse the performances that were planned for the final day. "Tomorrow morning's the Parade," she said. "Early start, remember! In the afternoon Oleg wants to show us his favourite Moscow church, and in the evening it's the Lenin Hills for the fireworks. Wednesday's a full programme as well, so now's the time to polish up your shows."

Groans: "We only have to walk it through, then rehearse the songs at the last minute. We know it *backwards*, Ellen!" The Moscow lot, used to performing in the studio already, didn't want a long rehearsal either. Ellen looked at Oleg. "Rebellion amidst the troops?" he asked, shrugging his shoulders. "You have wishes that we have not so far met?"

The Pentre Corach group shuffled uncomfortably. Megan was afraid someone would say they were missing *Neighbours* or wanted some decent night life.

Olwen spoke out. "Some of us were talking at lunch... It's just that we're right in the middle of everything here. We've done lots of sightseeing, but we're missing out on what's really going *on*."

"Yes!" Megan hadn't meant to launch in, but she did. "I mean – " She caught Oleg's gaze settling on her, and wavered – "Moscow's – well, it's sort of seething – someone said there's going to be some alternative demo tomorrow – " She couldn't stand Oleg's eyes any longer and turned to Ellen. "Sort of in revolt against the main parade... But we're just tourists..."

Olwen took over again. "What about Germany, and Berlin? We saw that bloke flash by – Krenz. What's going on? Is there any way we can find out?"

There were murmurs among the others. "It's all happening! We want to know!" Even Spock was nodding.

Ellen and Oleg muttered to each other in Russian. "You are right, Megan and Olwen," said Oleg. "We must discover some of what is happening. I have a friend in the east part of Berlin – his mother, she is very old, she has been allowed to go to the West. There are telephones, are there not, in the Salyut Hotel? Shall I now telephone my friend and ask him the news? I can try."

As they all crowded out through the studio doors, Megan and Riina gravitated towards Nadya and Mish.

"Why the hotel?" Megan asked. "Your flat's nearer, isn't it, Riina?"

"No good," Nadya said dismissively. "Only Moscow."

"What d'you mean, only Moscow?" asked Mish.

"Telephones. For far places, for abroad places, we must make the booking – then, middle of the night suddenly, there is a line! You foreign visitors, you can telephone more easy in special hotels."

But "more easy" didn't mean easy. They got to the hotel, waited twenty minutes for Oleg to get attention at the desk, half an hour more for him to

110

convince the woman that he was attached to British guests staying at the hotel, and nearly an hour after that to get an overseas line. Meanwhile the group kicked their heels and got in the way of hotel guests and porters, and Ellen tried to fill in their picture of life in a divided Germany. "In the East, they sit there watching West German TV – it all looks like *Dallas* and *Dynasty* – so it's up sticks and get there by any means possible. Some embassies have got hundreds of people climbing over the walls to get in..."

Jim broke into Ellen's lecture and spoke up. "But couldn't Mr – er – Krenz just open the Berlin Wall and let people through?"

"No!" Nina turned to him. "It is not possible, Jim. To open, that would be the end of the Communism!"

When Oleg finally got through, they crowded round the phone. He was chatting away in German. "How many languages does he *speak*, for God's sake?" muttered Abi.

When he put down the phone, he turned round. "I knew that his mother was old and ill," he said quietly. "She died last week. Without seeing her son again. He tells me that someone has written on the Wall – 'It should be easier to visit one's family than to go to the moon.'"

Megan, walking back to the flat with Riina, wondered what on earth she was going to wear to the party at Nina's. It'd have to be her black sweatshirt and the flowery skirt with tassels round the edge – flimsy and short, she'd perish with cold on the way, but Nina's flat was bound to be steaming hot. If only they could go and watch Kostya!

She tried not to look at Riina putting on a calf-length waisted dress that Megan's gran would have called a frock. When they caught each other's eye she said awkwardly, "Fashions seem to be different in Britain and the Soviet Union."

"We think it important we be feminine," answered Riina.

"But women here go out to work all the time, don't they? Surely they need to be practical, not wear stilettos?"

Riina laughed. "Megan! What clothes we wear is for the boys, of course! Is it not thus with you also?"

"But don't you ever wear jeans, like Nadya?"

Riina's face fell. "I cannot acquire the blue-jeans. They cost so dear, and one must find the right persons to sell them. Soon we go home to Tallinn, therefore we must not have trouble." Megan made a mental note to leave her jeans behind in Riina's drawer. Mum would be proud of her generosity and instantly buy her some more.

Before the party, they had to buy a present for Nina. They walked under the street-lamps to the market and found it still open. Wind swirled round the tower-blocks, nearly blowing them off their feet, and dust flew in their faces.

The problem wasn't deciding what Nina's taste was, or even whether they could afford it, but what was available. The market stalls were practically empty. What about a bag of apples? They were battered and bruised, the kind you'd throw out back home. Knitted hats? Only children and old men wore them. Fur hats and ladies' boots – hardly appropriate. Eventually Riina chose the best of a few remaining pomegranates – "flown in by aeroplane from the Black Sea," the grizzled stall-holder told them – and a chrysanthemum each for Nina's parents.

"Nina's flat – is it like yours?" Megan asked as they walked on. She wanted to find out what Abi meant by "party apparatchik".

"Like, and not like. Nina is..."

"What – rich? Posh?"

"What is 'posh'? Her father and mother, they are friendly with the Communist Party."

"What difference does that make?"

"Every difference! You will see. Nina has much. Not like Nadya with black market. Nina has video machine which operates, she has new rock songs from the West, her parents have *dacha* by Black Sea for holidays, they can enable repairs to their apartment..."

"Because she's rich?"

Riina snorted. "Rich is nothing. Here, everything is 'connections'. You say all the time 'Yes' to the Party – then things are good for you."

"But that's corrupt!"

"I have not that word. Again, please, Megan?"

"Corrupt."

"Corr-rrupt. I will remember."

They walked on in silence. Megan tried to digest this. Then, "One more question, Riina. This party."

"Not Party, not corrupt, please. It makes anger in me."

"No, *this* party – Nina's party. What stuff will we be drinking? Vodka? Wine?"

"Oleg Stepanovich, he instructs us no alcohol. Until twenty-one years in Soviet Union, we drink no alcohol in public place. In private it is allowed. But my mother and father are…"

"Strict."

"Strict. I wish that parents of the boys also could be so strict."

The door to Nina's flat had three locks, like the Tormises', and a spyhole as well. The buzz of chatter from inside told them that most of the group had already arrived. Nina's father thanked them for the gifts and said he and his wife would be going out shortly "to leave the young to be young".

Nina's flat was certainly much better fitted out than Riina's. The sofa and chairs matched and seemed new, and the sofa wasn't the kind that converted into a bed. Jim was giving Nina a helping hand as if he were part of the scenery. Just now he was handing round platefuls of sticky cakes.

Soon all twelve pairs were packed into the living room. Nina's father put his head round the door with, "We go now! Be happy!"

No sooner had the front door shut than Vitya called for attention.

"Silent!" echoed Levan. The chattering stopped.

"Be happy! That is our order!" Vitya looked round at them, mimicking Oleg. "What sadness it is," he said, in mock misery, "the parents, the teachers cannot be present with us. But they say, 'You are the adult people now. You must entertain the guests.' So – that we do! We entertain as only Moscow entertain!"

He and Levan swung open their jackets. Hanging in inner pockets, two to each, were enormous bottles of vodka.

"*Nyet!*" cried Nina. Moving her bulk with the speed she'd shown in the studio, she went for Vitya with an agitated babble of Russian.

"What's she saying?" Megan asked Riina. Levan had taken Nina by the shoulders and firmly drawn her away.

"Russian boys," answered Riina gloomily. "I drink not. Boys, they must always drink. Will you drink?"

Megan decided she was liable enough to panic without alcohol lowering her inhibitions, so she restricted herself to tea from the electric samovar – or rather, tea from the teapot weakened with water from the samovar.

Nina's video recorder did work, and she insisted the curtains were drawn in case someone outside saw it and was tempted to burglary. Everyone cheered when the picture flickered on, then jeered when the only video cassette turned out to be an old film about the mad monk Rasputin in the last days of the Tsars.

Whether fiddling with the video recorder or pouring from the samovar, Jim was at Nina's side. Megan noticed Vitya nudging Levan with a gesture of his head towards them.

Levan approached Jim with a bottle of vodka. "You will drink, Jim?"

"Er – no, thanks all the same."

Levan wouldn't be put off. "To give pleasure to us, your duty will be to drink."

"We men, we drink," urged Vitya. "For our strength, for our manliness we drink."

Megan turned her back on the humiliation of Jim. It was too predictable. Why did Ellen choose him? It must have been pity, or pressure from his father, a school governor. She went over to the huddle where Mish and Olwen were in hoots of laughter over Masha's fantasies of the British. "But in my thoughts you are so elegant – so serious – your Shakespeare, your Keats, your Byron, such poets are romantic in all your hearts…"

When Megan next glanced at Jim and Nina they were sitting close on the sofa, vodka glasses in hand. Levan was by the door chatting up Annest, who looked stunning as usual in a silk blouse belted loosely over her slim jeans, with Abi hovering near by offering cigarettes. Most of the lads smoked, and the coarse smell of Russian tobacco began to pervade the room. Tie and Spock were trying out "What D'You Call a One-Eyed Dinosaur" on Mike and Sasha. Vitya was still hanging round Nina and Jim, plying them with vodka.

Meredydd, snuffling with cold, and Seriozha joined Megan and Mish and the rest, and for a while they compared the different rock groups currently hitting the charts at home. Over their shoulders came Tie's "D'yerthink-'e-saurus!"

116

followed by confused "ums" and "ers" from Sasha and Mike.

Megan glanced at the sofa. Jim had his arm round Nina, and she was gazing into his eyes as if he were God's gift to the female Russian soul. Masha giggled. "Your Jim – he is the man of Nina's moment!"

Vitya, leaving the bottle beside the happy pair, strolled over. He knelt beside Masha and put his arm round her shoulders. "Ah, now our Nina learns what love is!" he said, then came out with some Russian. Masha blushed, and Nadya and Seriozha shook with laughter.

"Nina," Vitya explained in English, "is our most favourite person, because she reminds of our favourite person. Of whom do I speak? Of course, of our darling, dead-as-the-doornail Mr Leonid Brezhnev. Nina has looks of him, think you not?" The Russians fell about. Megan racked her brains to remember what Mr Brezhnev looked like – square-shaped, with thick eyebrows, like Nina?

Nina and Jim were helping themselves liberally to Vitya's vodka. Nina swung her feet up on the sofa and reclined ever more intimately on Jim. Megan saw Annest refuse another of Abi's cigarettes and cut herself loose from Levan, walk over to the sofa, and bend to pick up the bottle.

"Hey!" said Jim. "Leave that there! He gave it to us, whassisname – it's all ours, he said!"

"You've had enough, Jim," said Annest. She said it low so as not to shame him. But a hush had fallen on the room and everyone heard.

"Leave the bottle!" ordered Nina in a high-pitched voice. "This be my country, my Moscow. I will drink if I will, and so will he!"

Annest pursed her lips, put the bottle down and went back to the door. The rest broke into embarrassed chat.

Llyr decided to teach the Russians how to sing Welsh Penyllion in the correct harmonies. "Remember, Penyllion is not choral shinging," he instructed. He shook off Tom, who was urging him to teach them "Cwm Rhondda" instead. "Who are your lead shingers? Mike – and Masha." The bottles were almost empty. What hadn't gone down Jim and Nina had disappeared mostly into the Russian boys. But the Moscow group were used to vodka; Jim, Llyr and the others were not.

Megan gave Mish's arm a squeeze and indicated that she was going to the bathroom. Mish extricated herself and came too.

Mish didn't seem alarmed. "Men!" she said.

"But what if one of them's sick all over Nina's carpet?"

"They'll fall into a drunken stupor soon enough, just you see."

"How'll they get home? We can't get a taxi without the Russians' help, and they're all canned out of their minds…"

"Don't panic, Meggo. The girls are sober, they'll know what to do. How about Gentleman Jim and Nina, then? Trouble is, contraception's almost non-existent in the Soviet Union, so Nadya says. D'you know what they call Russian condoms? 'Galoshes'! And you can't get any even if you wanted to."

"How do they manage? Hardly any of this lot seem to have brothers or sisters."

"Abortion, so it seems. Half a dozen's the average, per woman. Imagine!"

"Mish! Did Nadya tell you that?"

"Yep. I got her on to it when I fetched a tampon out of my bag and she asked 'What is that thing, Michelle?' When I told her, she collapsed. 'That truly is heaven, Michelle – woman's heaven!'"

"They don't *have* them?"

"Nope. Hey – what's that row?"

They rushed back to the living room. The door was blocked by Tie and Llyr clutching each other for support between the door-posts. But Mish and Megan, peering between them, could see what was going on.

It was a slow handclap. Everyone was standing or sitting round the edges of the room, clapping rhythmically and urging on the two in the centre.

Jim and Nina were like a slowly moving erotic sculpture. They stood, arms entwined, lips and hips pressed together, Jim's trouser belt undone and hanging loose, Nina's lurex top dragged off one broad shoulder. His hands started to stroke one of her dome-like breasts. As Megan stared, he began unzipping himself and propelling Nina towards the sofa. Jim's hand pulled the lurex lower, revealing a copious bra. Nina hitched her skirt further up her thighs and the pair of them, with a heavy bounce, fell on to the sofa.

Oh almighty God, thought Megan. They're going to do it. They're actually going to do it, with all of us looking on. She caught sight of Olwen and

Masha, pinned to the wall over the other side of the room. Their faces were twin pictures of disgust.

Bang! An unidentifiable noise came from along the hall. Megan turned. Was someone being sick in the bathroom – had they collapsed on the floor?

Bang! Someone was at the front door.

She grabbed Mish. "Who — ?"

No one else had heard. Mish started along the hall. Terrified, Megan followed.

Mish tried to negotiate three complicated locks. Who was it? Neighbours? Police, to arrest for affray?

Mish managed the last lock and pulled the door open. Mrs Haigh stood there, with Annest and Mari behind.

Mrs Haigh swept in. "Just *what* is going on-a? Some kind of orgy?"

Mari followed her down the hall. Annest stood helplessly with Megan and Mish. "We went to the Salyut. Tried to find Ellen – she was nowhere to be seen. Abi's mum said, 'In some bar with the Baranov man, most likely.' There was no stopping her."

"I bet there wasn't," said Mish. "Let's view the damage."

The living room doorway had cleared for Mrs Haigh to pass through. The teenagers pressed themselves harder into the walls and furniture. Nina, her face streaked with tears, was standing up and rearranging her bra and lurex top. Jim stood apart from her. He was breathing heavily and clutching his flies. Then, with a suddenness that surprised Megan, he interrupted Mrs Haigh's tirade by throwing up at her feet.

CHAPTER SEVEN

We were living in the shadow of the worst danger in the history of any people – the divorce between its outward and its inner life.

Yevtushenko, *A Precocious Autobiography*

They shuffled uncomfortably as they gathered in the half darkness next morning, ready to set off for the Revolution Parade. Only Nina's square face was lit up. Did her mother have herbal cures for hangovers as well as bad backs? She bubbled with chat and instructions. No one took any notice except Abi, who looked embarrassed.

Jim was missing. According to Dima, it was "necessary for him to remain in his bed".

Megan and Riina had hardly spoken half a sentence since they woke up. The air was dank and raw. Is this what I came to Moscow for, Megan asked herself – chilled hangovers before dawn?

Sylvia paced impatiently up and down: several people were late, including the Haighs and the Garth Joneses – late, for this most vital of Soviet ceremonies! Ellen stood alone, eyes fixed on her clipboard. Oleg was deep in Russian talk with Mike and Seriozha. Levan was peering down the road, probably for Annest, who'd still be administering her eyeliner.

121

Megan's throat felt tight and dry. She must have caught Meredydd's cold. That meant she'd be coughing and spluttering through the Parade, and tonight's fireworks, and most likely the rest of the week. If only she and Riina had gone to the *Lysistrata* rehearsal last night! Would they get to the performance? Did she want to face Kostya with her nose all red and stuffed-up? Did Riina want her to see Kostya again, or would she make excuses to stay away from the theatre till the Brits left for home?

Home. Cottage, school, Dafydd. As she stamped her feet in thick socks and Doc Martens she had a sudden sense of Dafydd – his high cheekbones, the mole just below his left eye, the fingernails cut very short except for the ones he played his guitar with. The times since that Sunday when they'd sat, arms round each other, saying nothing, and he hummed tunes she didn't know, till she accused him of droning, then he'd say, "I wasn't humming! I never hum!" and they'd wrestle till the wrestling turned to kisses. He'd learnt to kiss properly since they were together last time. Where had he learnt – who from? She didn't mind.

What mood would Abi's mum be in today? She was probably opposed on principle to celebrating a Communist Revolution. But last night they'd all been amazed by Mrs Haigh. She'd ignored Jim and Nina's state of undress. She'd sent Jim home with Dima (who was sober), she'd told Abi and Masha to help Nina to bed, then she'd asked for a bucket from the kitchen and cleaned up Jim's vomit herself.

At last the Haighs and the Garth Joneses emerged from the hotel, and they could see Annest and Sonya hurrying down the road. Annest walked straight past Levan, hissing at him, "Stop drinking, and grow up!" Ellen ticked everyone's names off as they filed on to the coach.

Mrs Haigh was absorbed in conversation with Mrs Garth Jones. So, there was to be no lecture. She'd done her duty, she'd brought the young people under control. Except for absent Jim, it seemed the incident was closed.

"We'll be in Red Square on November 7th," Megan had told Mum and Dad. "Watch the news. You know where that row of fur-hatted old men stand, on the parapet above Lenin's Tomb? We'll be just the other side of the square. I'll wave my red flag and shout 'Gorby for Number 10!'"

But Sylvia didn't take them to Red Square. There were so many soldiers and dignitaries and heroes of the Soviet Union to be fitted in, she explained, there wasn't room for tourists like themselves. She gave them each a balloon – "Balloons!" muttered the lads. "Like toddlers!" – as they drove along in the gathering light. When they arrived, she shepherded them through lines and lines of parked coaches to another vast square, where she arranged them along the pavement.

They stood, and they waited. The whole crowd waited. Even the policemen on duty lounged about, chatting and smoking. Little stalls were selling miniature red flags and Russian dolls, and along the road there was a makeshift buffet offering Soviet Pepsi, chocolate éclairs and plastic cups of tea.

When they got bored with waiting, the Pentre Corach gang wandered among the hordes of other tourists, listening to people babbling in every language under the sun. The Welskis reacted by chattering loudly about Eisteddfodau and rugby matches at Parc yr Arfau Caerdydd. "Exhibitionists!" accused Abi.

A troupe of American clowns provided a diversion. One walked on stilts, his trouser-legs starred and striped like the US flag. He offered them stickers urging them to "Visualize World Peace", so Spock stuck one on his torn anorak next to "Welsh Rugby Players Do It in the Mud".

Megan was glad of a mug of tea. It soothed her throat and helped her pretend her cold would come to nothing. Had she got enough tissues with her? Could you buy decent paper hankies in Moscow? Not if their coarse loo-paper was anything to go by.

To distract her attention, she gazed at the squat khaki-grey missile-carriers in the square. Polished up for the occasion, they looked almost like toys. Some were even tied to their carriers with red ribbon. Every so often a balloon would fly loose in the wind and a soldier would crawl between the wheels of his missile-carrier to rescue it.

"I suppose they've got things like this targeted on Cardiff and Liverpool," said Olwen, "but you can't believe it, can you?"

"Some deterrent, eh!" said Abi. Her parents had disappeared to the other end of the line and

she was having a quick puff. Nina stood beside her, looking disapproving.

"You don't believe all that crap, do you?" asked Olwen. Megan knew about Olwen's politics – her mum had been to Greenham Common. Megan's parents had talked to her at a parents' evening, and Dad had made some comment like, "Fancy her being safely married. I didn't think any of that lot were."

"The bomb's done more for world peace than your precious Greenham women," said Abi.

"Oh? What if it had gone off? We'd none of us be standing here now. Mr Gorbachev wants a nuclear-free world – doesn't he, Nina?"

They turned to Nina. Megan waited for a blast of apparatchik-speak.

But Nina looked confused. "We in Soviet Union fight always for peace," she muttered.

"Oh?" said Abi. "So why all this, then?" – waving at the missiles.

"Shut up, Abi," said Olwen. "You know Gorby's trying to get rid of them. You don't want our stuff aiming straight for people like Oleg, do you?"

Abi blushed, and Megan stared at her. It wasn't like Abi to give up so easily. Don't say this visit was going to convert her to CND?

At last someone started to make speeches in Russian over the loud-speaker, and the missile-carriers started up their engines with a fog of exhaust. They lumbered off, urged on by a mammoth poster of waving Lenin, and headed for Red Square.

Beyond the missile-carriers far over to the right stood a queue of ordinary Russian citizens. At first Megan assumed they were onlookers, but then they started to wave banners as well as balloons and she realized they were part of the parade itself. When the Missile Parade ended, the People Parade began. Slowly the procession edged forward, everyone waving flags, banners and balloons: men, women, children, booted and scarved and fur-hatted – on and on and on.

Do they mean it? Megan wondered. Are they sincerely celebrating the Communist Revolution? She moved towards Sylvia, hoping to pluck up courage to ask. Would she be offended by a question like that?

Ah – Mish was asking something. "How many d'you think there are in these processions?"

"I cannot say. Many hundreds of thousands."

"And do they come here because they want to?"

"Of course! Who would compel them?" Then the official face softened. "Perhaps some come from habit only. It is a pleasant holiday. Normal life ceases for us, because November 7th is special."

"How long will it go on being special?" asked Olwen.

"I do not know," replied Sylvia. "How can any person know what will happen in the future?"

Lunch was a celebratory affair. Each place was marked with a tiny red flag, and bottles of champagne stood on the central table. The first course, lying ready on each plate, was a small

126

portion of segmented white fish. "Sturgeon!" said Mrs Haigh, impressed.

"Hey, Eilen," called Tie, "can we have some of that champagne?"

"No, you can not!"

"Perhaps we may keep the bottles for the banquet on our final evening?" suggested Oleg.

"We'll give them to Sylvia as a present," said Ellen coldly. "I want no more alcohol in the Pentre Corach camp, thank you." Megan noticed that she put Mrs Garth Jones between herself and Oleg at the central table.

She and Riina sat with Mish and Nadya, who were back in their own jeans today but wore each other's jackets, scarves and gloves. "Nadya," said Mish as they downed the sturgeon in a couple of bites, "where did the vodka come from last night? Have Vitya and Levan got a secret cellar?"

"Vitya and Levan? No. Adults only have such secrets." Nadya was glancing uneasily at Riina.

"Who?" persisted Mish. "Their parents?"

"Maybe, maybe. Who knows."

Riina wanted to change the subject. "It is necessary for you to understand our teacher Oleg Stepanovich," she said. "A short biography would perhaps be useful to you?"

"Yes," said Megan. "Fill us in."

Riina scribbled in her little notebook, *Fill us in*, then looked at Nadya. "How is good to begin?"

Sonya and Masha and Tanya were coming round with platefuls of meat and potatoes. Megan and Mish gazed at the size of the meat chunks – twice as big as anything they'd seen since

Heathrow. The Moscow group fell on their platefuls and gobbled all the meat before touching a single potato.

Nadya leaned forward and spoke in a discreet undertone. "Oleg Stepanovich is, um, fighter. Champion. Was."

"*Fighter?*"

"With swords. It is good – not for killing – like dance, understand?"

Mish got it. "Fencing?"

"It is so," murmured Riina. "Then he gained employment with the theatre, ensuring actors may fight without wounds to their bodies..."

"A fight-arranger..."

"And he was so excellent that he became to act, in addition."

Megan glanced over to Oleg's table. He was explaining something earnestly to Masha, leaning forward over his plate, eyes alive, gesticulating with his knife. She couldn't see Masha's face, just a chunk of meat poised in mid-air on her fork. "Actor plus fight-arranger? In that case," she asked, "how did he sink so low as teaching?"

"Ah," said Nadya. "It is no employment for a man, this teaching, is it not? That is our question, too, about Oleg Stepanovich."

"We hear it is the unhappiness in marriage," said Riina. "Problems of love – you know – they happen."

At the far table, Oleg had stopped gesticulating. His hair flopped over his face, and he was picking at a pile of tepid potatoes as if his concentration had fallen on to the plate like a stone.

128

"Somehow it was," Nadya was saying, "that the life of Oleg Stepanovich breaks into a thousand pieces."

"As you too will break the life of sad Yuri, Nadya," said Riina.

Nadya screwed up her face. "Yuri interests himself only in the politics. Today he has his own parade – for his Mr Yeltsin – for saying bad things about *perestroika*..."

Megan broke in. She needed to bring the talk round to Kostya. "Listen. D'you think we can get to *Lysistrata*? We missed the dress rehearsal – they really seemed to want us to go. What would Ellen say if we bunked off whatever they've fixed tomorrow evening? D'you want to go, Mish?"

"It'd be fantastic. Go on, Nadya," pleaded Mish. "I know you're trying to throw Yuri off, you beast, but – "

"I suspect you are fancying of Yuri for yourself, Michelle!"

Mish kicked her under the table. "I'm not! I only want to go to some decent theatre instead of all this ballet and folk stuff. Anyway, I asked Ellen what we were doing tomorrow evening and she said, 'Shopping in the Salyut Hotel for souvenirs.'"

"Ah, the Beriozhka shopping," said Riina. "It is a duty of tourists to spend their valuable currency in this way."

"Well, I vote for *Lysistrata*," declared Mish. "Who's coming with me?"

"I am, for a start," said Megan. "Riina?"

Riina shrugged her shoulders and wrinkled her

forehead. "Of course I must act the good hostess. And you, Nadya?"

"So much choice I have! OK, I come."

The Yelokhovsky Cathedral wasn't Sylvia's choice for a visit, not even Ellen's, but Oleg's.

They went by Metro. "I was born near to this place," Oleg explained as they crowded round him and hung on and swayed in the packed noisy train. "And again I live near to it now. See, when we arrive, all around the sacred building stand trolley-buses. No persons were permitted to worship their God in this cathedral, and the surrounding area was taken for a trolley-bus park. Now persons can go, worship, sing, marry, be baptized, have the burials."

Megan blew her nose and looked round their group. Who was a churchgoer? Hardly any. Abi's parents, with Abi dragged along at Christmas and Easter ... Tom and Mari were Chapel, but only for weddings and funerals... Maybe Jim was churchy, but he wasn't here.

Mrs Haigh leant over her shoulder. "Megan dear, what a frightful snuffle. I've got some cold remedies back at the hotel. I'll bring them to the fireworks tonight."

"Oh! Thanks, Mrs Haigh! That's really nice of you." Great – she'd be able to sit through *Lysistrata* without snorting like a pig, and look good for Kostya. Little did Abi's mum know how generous she was being.

The cathedral was a place of arches, domes and columns, freshly painted in aquamarine and white and topped with tiny crosses of gold. Ellen gathered them round her under the trolley-bus wires. "I want your full attention. Unlike our cathedrals, there are no pews here, no choir-stalls, no organ. The atmosphere is informal, and you can wander around even if services are going on. But there will be Russians here who are seeing these icons and worshipping for the very first time. You will behave with the utmost respect."

Inside it was dim, but glowing with gold and with the hundreds of candles that hung in candelabras in front of painted icons. People were lighting candles, melting the base and placing them for a prayer. Old women in scarves were rubbing the gold and brass with soft cloths, tourists took photos, and there was a murmur of voices in the silence.

The gleaming gold took Megan's breath away. Ahead of her, under the dome, there was a wall of it, encasing icon after icon – Madonna and Child, Christ in Majesty, Apostles, Bible stories. Each painting was warmed into life by the shimmering of the candles.

She turned to see where the rest of the group had gone. They were a little way away, with their backs to her, and were staring at a ceremony going on in a side aisle. It was a funeral. In the centre of the aisle lay a red plush coffin, open, and inside lay an old woman, dressed in black and white and surrounded by flowers. Megan watched, not shocked but fascinated. When the prayers were over, a man sounded a note on a tuning fork, a small group started to sing, and two men reverently put the coffin lid in place.

Almost immediately something started to

happen in the far aisle. At first Megan couldn't see why they'd gathered. She saw Ellen and Oleg standing, together now, at the back. The funeral choir reappeared on a balcony, and a bearded priest emerged from nowhere leading a young man. The young man walked through the congregation and led back a young woman dressed in simple everyday clothes and a headscarf. This was a wedding.

Tears stung in Megan's eyes. These church services weren't elaborate or routine. They were hard won, and filled with deep hunger.

She glanced around to take in the shimmering gold again. There was a candelabra hanging in front of a Madonna and Child just across the main aisle. Kostya was standing there, looking through the candles at the icon behind.

He held an unlit candle, but he didn't place it in the candelabra straight away. He was gazing at the icon as though it held something vital for him – a gift, information, help. His thin face took a warm glow from the candlelight, and she could see dark shadows beneath the bones of his cheek and under his chin.

Then he relaxed, put the candle to a flame, lit it, melted its base and put it firmly in place. He half smiled to himself, stuck his hands in his pockets and went on standing there, looking satisfied. She wanted to go over to him, but more powerfully than that, she wanted not to disturb him. He might have come here wanting to see her and Riina. But once he was here, his whole attention had focussed on lighting his candle and thinking of the person he had lit the candle for.

He looked slowly up at the icon, and then moved his gaze over towards her.

Still the half smile, unchanged. The smile was for the candlelit Madonna and for her, Megan, as well. He turned back and looked again at the icon. Then he walked over.

"Maygann."

"Hello, Kostya."

"You are here."

"You lit a candle."

"For *Babushka*. A candle by me, to my grandmother."

"That's lovely."

"She was for me a mother always." Like Dafydd, with his *nain* and *taid*. "My true mother – " he made a dismissive gesture.

"Your *babushka* – she's dead now?"

"*Da* – yes. She died before she need. She suffered."

Megan's eyes stung again, and her heart thudded, hurting her. Suffered! When had she suffered, or her parents, or her grandparents? Cattle-trucks – seige – Siberia – censorship – hunger. Nothing in her experience could compare.

"Maygann – " Kostya was alert suddenly. He turned away from the candlelit icon and his grandmother. He was making plans. "Yuri, he is out there. He comes not in, he likes not churches. He needs cigarette. He wishes to see, you know, Nadya. Come you out there? With Nadya – and, yes, Riina also?"

* * *

133

Yuri stood in the cold, puffing away on his cigarette. As Kostya and the four girls came out of the cathedral he ground his stub into the dust and walked towards them.

"You come! Last night, you did not come. To rehearsal." He made a fist of one gloveless hand and held it with the other, cracking his knuckles loud. "Why did you not?"

"It's awkward, honestly," said Mish, "getting away from the rest. There was this party – "

"Party? Good? Lots of fun?" He was asking Nadya, meaning, what men were you with?

"Lots of vodka," said Megan. "You should have seen Jim with Nina..."

"I know not these people," said Yuri. "Nadya..." and he went off into a torrent of Russian.

"*Pazhal'sta*, Yuri!" said Kostya. "Please, English for the guests! He is this morning at the politics – he forgets politenesses."

Yuri retorted rudely, "You be there, Kostya, if you wish a good reform in our country. Our bread is truth! The reform presently – it is no good, not quick sufficient for us. Gorbachev – he talks, but nothing happen! He is a liar, like all. They are all liars."

"*Nyet*, Yuri," said Nadya, nudging Riina. "We need person like Mr Brezhnev now. That I believe. We Russians, there must be for us a strong man, or there becomes... How you say?"

"Anarchy?" suggested Mish.

"Anarchy. With our Mr Brezhnev, at least we could know every tomorrow, know the future! Now, every day, is so much uncertain!"

Yuri, cracking his knuckles again, turned on Riina and Megan. "You see, you see how it is that we do not move? Our people are slaves, all slaves! How shall we make our democracy from a nation of slaves?" Then Nadya kicked him. "You...!" he spluttered at her.

"She was teasing," said Mish.

"What is 'teasing'?" Yuri whipped a little dictionary out of his pocket and looked it up. "Understood! Nadya – always she is teasing!" And the two of them began a fierce Russian argument, with Mish trying in English to soothe them.

"Kostya..." Riina took Megan's arm and took a hesitant step towards him.

"Riina..." Kostya turned, and Megan sensed him switching on his charm. "So good you are, to inform me of everywhere you are coming this week. So is it easy for me to see. Our *Lysistrata* the next day, Wednesday. You come?"

"We will come," said Riina quietly. "We must make it understood with our teachers, but we will come. Is it not right, Megan?"

"That's right." Megan had to turn aside to take a tatty tissue out of her pocket and blow her nose. "The wind – it makes my nose run."

Kostya was all consideration. "You wish inside cathedral once again? To become warm?"

"No, no. They'll be coming out in a minute anyway."

"Your group comes? Ah – then must I say quickly what I must say."

He came close. Megan caught a glimpse of the cat-like specks in his grey eyes. Kostya the cat.

135

What is a cat like? He's cold and hungry, he comes to you for food and comfort. Then he walks away.

"Tonight," he said, "you go to fireworks of course. But to which fireworks go you?"

"To the Lenin Hills, before the University," said Riina.

"Ah – the best. I too be there. Yuri, for him not possible. He has chief husband-part in our play. Uncle Vanya must instruct him. But I, I be there. There be some time, to walk a little, talk a little." He leaned towards Megan as he said it.

Riina said hurriedly, "It is most kind you are, Kostya. It makes our friends from Wales happy to meet so interesting students like yourself. It makes Moscow a memorable time for them. Does it not, Megan?"

"Oh – yes, it does." Megan began to feel panic coming on. Her heart thumped. What was in Kostya's mind? What was he planning? "Look, Ellen and the others will be wondering where we are..." She moved a foot towards the cathedral door.

"They are such fireworks, you have not seen such..." Kostya gestured hugeness.

"I'm sure, yes, I'm really looking forward to them. Riina, maybe we ought to go back in?"

"Yes, we must," said Riina.

"This night, I see you, both." Kostya took first Megan's hand, then Riina's. "Until."

"Until," said Megan.

Riina said, "*Do svidanya*, Kostya."

They left the others still arguing and turned to go back into the cathedral. Megan's heartbeat began to subside.

136

In the doorway an old beggar was standing, bent and dishevelled. He was holding out a small wooden bowl in a twisted hand. Riina stopped by him and the bowl jerked expectantly. But Riina took no notice of the beggar. She spoke to Megan in an urgent whisper. "You may have him, Megan! I have certainty he likes you much. Please, have him – then I will be free of my liking!"

"But Riina – I can't! We go home on Friday! It's ridiculous!"

"Say to me, Megan, honest – do you like him? Do you fancy?"

"Of course I do. But it's nonsense – there's no time – there's Dafydd – I couldn't – "

Riina took Megan's hand in both of hers. "Thank you, Megan. Thank you. If you like and he likes, there is not a possibility for me. I will be kind to you, and I will be good to me too, for not loving a Russian boy." She let go of Megan, put her hand in her pocket, took out as many coins as she could hold and poured them into the astonished beggar's trembling bowl.

All the way home Megan argued with her. When they got to the Metro platform she pulled her into a carriage away from the others so that they could argue in privacy. "On Friday I'll be *gone*, Riina – then you can have him to yourself! What does he mean, 'walk a little, talk a little'? The three of us, or what? What'll Ellen say if I go wandering off? In any case, I'm going out with Dafydd, we're together, I don't want to get *involved*..."

Riina was now quite composed. "Maybe

Dafydd is finding some joy while you are absent, Megan? Fear not, Kostya will be your English gentleman absolutely. He will take care of you. A good Russian boy always takes care of a girl."

"But —"

"Megan, no trouble is caused for your boy at home. Kostya will be unable to come to Wales, this week, the next week, the after week. Is not so?"

Megan's head was hot with arguing. She took off her yellow hat and shook her hair out. "You're offering him to me, because of *politics*! I mean, putting politics before passion! They told me Russians were such *romantic* people!"

"Russian persons – *they* be romantic in front of the politics. I am a *Estonian* person. I put first the country."

"I don't feel at all romantic, I've got a stinking cold and I always look revolting with a cold…"

Her brain seethed like a cauldron. The image of Kostya's candlelit face in front of the icon surfaced again and again. But flashing up beside it came the question – "Does he really prefer me to Riina? Or am I just a passport to the West?" Nadya – *the West is all she lives for. Kostya also, he wishes to be there, the West.* Was that his aim, to exchange his rabbit-hutch in Moscow for a stone cottage in the Clwyd hills? Then, when the cat has got what he wants, he'll walk away, off to London's golden pavements, doss-houses, the cardboard city under Waterloo Bridge…

Fantasizing again. Fantasy, that was her trouble. Like telling Riina those porky-pies about her family.

She realized they'd passed Sportivnaya Station and gone over the clattering river bridge and as far as University Station without saying a single word. Only two more stations to go.

"Riina," she said.

"Megan?"

"My family – they're very ordinary folks, actually. Dad's only a teacher, he's not an athlete or anything. Well, he's not a bad runner, but… And Mum doesn't paint for the National Gallery, she's only sold half a dozen pictures to friends. And Kate, she lives a normal life, she's not bedridden or anything. What I mean is, I was exaggerating."

"*Exaggerate.*" Riina flicked through her dictionary. "Ah! I understand. I too, Megan. My affection for Kostya. I exaggerate it. We must be truthful, yes? Your family are ordinary family – I like ordinary family. Kostya is not too special to me – Kostya is special to you. OK, all is OK."

CHAPTER EIGHT

What if he should take it into his head to make you happy in spite of yourself?

Pushkin, *Dubrovsky*

Jim was still missing when they gathered for the firework display. There was a buzz of anxiety. Nina and Abi had been to Dima's, and found Dima's mother most concerned because Jim hadn't emerged the whole day. Might Abi talk him into life? Abi had gone in and stood uncomfortably beside his sofa-bed, but Jim kept his face turned to the wall.

Mrs Haigh was telling Ellen they should phone Jim's home. Ellen was doubtful – Mrs Haigh insisted – but when they went into the hotel they were told there was no line free. Mrs Haigh muttered, "I get through to my sister in Canada as if she were in Holywell-a!" Ellen wondered if a special friend of Jim's could go and see him. But Jim didn't have a special friend.

Olwen was anxious about something else. "This currency business – Russians having to give ten roubles now in exchange for every pound sterling. I've been wondering, Oleg – what will that mean for your return trip? I mean, will anyone be able to afford to come to Wales?"

"That is our thought, too," answered Oleg. "Many problems arise from this. Much consideration must be given. All are present now, yes? We will go for the bus. No, don't trouble about tickets. I have books of tickets."

They were just moving off towards the bus stop when a woman ran down the steps, calling to them. Oleg caught Ellen's arm. "She is saying, they have a line. We can telephone to Britain."

Ellen frowned. "I'm not sure about this. What are we going to say to the Haydocks? I mean, it's — "

Mrs Haigh, Nina nodding at her elbow, interrupted her. "He's behaving very oddly. Maybe he's allergic to alcohol. They'd be able to advise... Oh, that reminds me. Megan needed first aid for her cold. Megan? Here you are." She handed over two packets. "Capsules or pills, take your choice."

"Thanks a lot, Mrs Haigh. I'll take some now." She'd always been able to swallow pills without water.

"Have you got enough paper tissues with you? No child ever has enough tissues, in my experience."

"Er, no, actually, I could do with a few more if you've got some spare." Mrs Haigh handed over a wad from her coat pocket. "Thanks ever so much."

Ellen was impatient about the phone call question. "But, Mrs Haigh, why didn't Dima's parents just call the doctor?"

"Yelyena," said Oleg, "you are still innocent

141

about this Soviet Union of ours. Here we do not
call a doctor without an envelope of roubles beside
the telephone."

"Bribery?" Mrs Haigh was horrified.

"I am sorry to give you this shock, Mrs Haigh.
But it is how it is."

"Look, it's after half past eight." Ellen,
uncharacteristically, was pleading with them. "If
we don't get a move on we'll miss the fireworks.
And it'll still only be half past five in Britain – the
Haydocks won't be back from work. Let's wait till
tomorrow morning."

Megan pressed a capsule out of its foil wrapper.
She'd take a couple of capsules, and a couple of
pills as well, just to make sure.

At the Lenin Hills the atmosphere was festive.
Russian mothers and *babushkas* clutched children
by the hand, fathers strode with toddlers on their
shoulders, young couples hurried hand in hand to
get to the scene of the fireworks by the stroke of
nine.

Megan and Riina and the rest of the gang
hurried too. Behind them a full moon rose above
the University's floodlit towers, and a few stars
twinkled. "How long will the fireworks go on
for?" Megan asked Ellen. Would Kostya find them
among the crowds?

"How long, Oleg?" Ellen asked.

"I do not know," Oleg replied. "It depends how
many they shoot."

"Shoot?" said Abi, coming up behind Ellen and
Oleg.

"It is not like your Guy Fawkes, Abigail. We do not have many, many little fireworks."

"You could whizz Catherine wheels on the side of the ski-jump..." Abi was excited.

"No, we have few extremely large fireworks. They shoot them from far, out of a... What was that word, Yelyena?"

"Cannon."

"Yelyena told me about your Guy Fawkes. Imagine, you celebrate the nearly blowing up of your Parliament!"

"We don't *celebrate* it," said Ellen. "Anyway, you've only just got a parliament. You wait, maybe you'll have your own Guy Fawkes one day. Look, it's dead on nine. Will they be —?"

Her word "punctual" was drowned by a Boom! The first cannon had fired. The crowd gave a spontaneous "Oooh!" But the sky stayed blank. Was it a dud?

It wasn't. The sky suddenly exploded with sparks – red, yellow and green – brighter and brighter and brighter – then each spark whitened until the air was light as day. You could see tendrils of smoke-trail behind the sparks, and a smoke-cloud reflected the glow of light.

Megan saw every face lit and smiling. Beside her stood a burly middle-aged man – he'd be a businessman, judging by the Japanese digital watch on his wrist – and even he let go his dignity and went "Oooh! Aaah!" like a child. For one moment, she thought, they can forget the queues and bribes and crimes and suffering and the uncertain future. Everyone is absorbed in the instant and the glow.

143

There was a crackle-crackle-crackle like chestnuts bursting in a bonfire, and the light faded quickly. Darkness again, and a hush of waiting. Then another Boom! – another moment of expectation – another exotic splash in the sky. Fade – wait – Boom! – and it happened again. Each boom produced a different combination of exploding colours.

On the other side of her, Megan could hear the Pentre Corach lads muttering. "Is this all we're getting? Rockets, rockets, rockets. What about a few bangers for a change – Roman candles? I've seen better in my back garden…" How dare they? The fireworks were brilliant, she'd never seen anything like them. Lads – British lads anyway – were always cynical, it spoilt everything. "Let's move over there," she murmured to Riina. "Nearer to the parapet." The nearer they were to the edge of the crowd, the more likely Kostya would see them.

"Look!" cried Riina as they got to the parapet. "And there – and there!"

All over Moscow, fireworks were being fired from other cannons just like here on the Lenin Hills. Boom! went their own cannon, and Boom! echoed the one away to their right. On the far side of the city, sparks appeared noiselessly from a cannon too distant to hear.

"Are there crowds like this at each place?" asked Megan.

"Yes, yes. And in every city of the Soviet Union."

"In Tallinn, as well? To celebrate the *Russian* Revolution?"

144

"This year, yes. But next year – perhaps we celebrate something else!"

The cannon boomed again, and in the darkness before the explosion Megan felt a hand placed on each of her shoulders. She froze. Sparks of pink, lime-green and lilac filled the air and grew into little balls of coloured light, then strengthened and bleached, turned white and evaporated. All the time, the hands went on exerting a little more pressure.

The cheers died away. The hand on her right shoulder lifted. "*Dobry vyecher*, Riina, Maygann," said Kostya. Megan's stomach lurched, and she turned round. Kostya's right hand transferred to Riina's shoulder, his left hand stayed on hers for another second.

She caught Riina's eye as they said hello. Riina was smiling diffidently.

"You're sure Uncle Vanya hasn't told you to learn your lines this evening?" Megan's head felt light, as if the fireworks had exploded all solid sense out of it. Or was it Abi's mum's cold remedies? Should she have taken both kinds?

Another firing of the cannon, another pause in the darkness, another glistening explosion. As it faded, Kostya said, "Ganuchka."

"What?"

"Russians, we make small names out from big names, big names out from small names. Nikolai, one names him Kolya. Our hero of theatre, Stanislavsky – I am as he, I am Konstantin. So they make me Kostya."

"Seriozha, short for Sergei," Riina reminded Megan.

145

"Anna, Anuchka. You are Maygann. I call you Ganuchka."

"Riina, Riinuchka," said Megan.

"*Da.*"

Cannon again. The three of them turned towards the sound. Kostya's hands returned to her shoulders, and he said in her ear, "Fall. Fall back." He had stepped closer to her. She leaned back a fraction, and he was there. By the time the coloured sparks began to whiten, she could feel the warmth of his body through her coat.

The smoke tendrils faded, the cloud dispersed to a haze in the clear black sky. The only sparks were stars, looking like leftover fireworks ready to start out for galactic spheres.

"Is over," said Kostya, stepping back and putting his hands in his pockets.

Everyone else realized it was over too, and applause sputtered through the crowd.

"It is for me the last November in Moscow," said Riina. "Next year – home."

"Next Friday – home," said Megan. Her back felt suddenly cold.

People slowly began to move away. Children still jumped with excitement and teenagers sang snatches of rude songs at each other. Elderly couples held hands as if the event stirred memories they'd rather face together.

The three of them walked with the crowd back towards the University. Megan noticed young couples trying to snatch a bit of privacy on park benches among the bushes beyond the lawns, but it was no use, some *mamushka* or *babushka* would

146

drag little Sasha or Masha to the bench to tie up a shoe-lace or button up a coat. There was no sign of the rest of the group.

"What's the plan, Riina?" asked Megan, swallowing the excitement in her throat. "What did Oleg and Ellen say we should do when the fireworks were over?"

"We catch back the bus towards our homes," answered Riina. "We then gather in Nina's apartment once more, for watching the Revolution parades on her television. So now we must see and find the others... There! Is Sasha and your Spock, with Mikhail and Tie. Mikhail!" She took a hurried step over to them.

"Riina —" Kostya stopped her, and said something hurriedly in Russian.

Megan saw Riina nodding agreement as if to say "That's all right". Could she go with Kostya? How? Her head was reeling like it had last Christmas when she'd drunk too much of Uncle Norman's elderberry wine. She ran and caught Riina's arm. "We ought to go with them, you know we ought, Riina, we ought, really..."

"I will go, Megan," said Riina firmly. "I will say, my mother did worry about your cold, and she came to find us here and took you to our home."

"Yes, yes," said Kostya.

"Kostya will bring you to our home, Megan, where I will soon be. Myself, I have no wish to watch television parades. Or you, Kostya? Or you, Megan?" She was walking away towards Tie and Spock. "Indeed no. I will see you. *Pakka.*"

* * *

Nervously she asked him what Riina had meant by "*Pakka*". What if it was a code word, something significant between her and Kostya – a warning that she ignored at her peril? No, he told her – it was ("how you say?") the word young people say when old people say farewell, adieu, *au revoir*. "Ah!" she said. "*Pakka!*" She could hardly look at his eyes.

"Not *pakka* now," said Kostya. "No farewell now. Now is hello. Hello, Ganuchka."

"Hello again, Kostya."

He took her hands, and all of a sudden she felt confident. Riina had said that Kostya, like a good Russian man, would look after her. She knew he would. And now his thin face was creased in a wide grin, a grin of mischief and freedom. Riina had said, "Everyone loves Kostya. He is not handsome – but fun? Yes and yes and yes." In the Arbat, in the cathedral, he'd been gentle, earnest, almost sombre. Now he was fun.

He let go of one of her hands and they ran back to the parapet overlooking the river and the city. "Moskva – our Moscow! She is at your feet!" Megan's head was now a hot-air balloon. She wouldn't have been surprised if she'd taken off and wafted across to the Kremlin.

Then, still running, Kostya led her away from the moonlit University, along a wide straight road to the left. "I will show you the whole things of Moscow, Ganuchka," he declared. Then he changed his mind – "Too long a way. I had wish to show you place of making films like *War and Peace*, but time is not enough."

"I thought *War and Peace* was a book?" she said breathlessly.

"Yes – you read?"

"No – I think it was done for TV…"

"You like TV, film? You know our wonderful film maker man, Tarkovsky?"

"No – d'you know Stephen Spielberg, he made *ET*?"

"*ET*, what is that, Ganuchka?"

But she couldn't explain, and back they went, round the moonlit University ("Where are we *going*, Kostya?") and along strange tree-lined streets till she had lost her bearings entirely.

She was dizzy and puffed, but she knew she had to pull in a thread of reality from somewhere. "Kostya – stop! Please! Listen."

He stopped instantly, took her hands and looked at her gravely. "Listen. I am listen." He put on a ham actor's serious face, lips pursed and eyebrows raised.

"Don't make me laugh. Look, I haven't got much time." He was fantastic, and he loved her. *What?* He fancied her. *OK*.

She said, finding the words with difficulty, "I've got to get back to Riina's flat before it gets late. You'll have to get back too, surely. Do you live with your parents? Whereabouts do you live?"

"I live near, near. It matters not what I do, Ganuchka."

"But it does matter. You know all about me, I know nothing about you." She must pull herself together. She put her hands round her yellow hat stuffed with hair and held her head to press some sense into it. "Tell me. How am I going to get home?"

"Easy. They take bus, therefore we take Metro. Metro is more quick than bus."

"Metro. I know – University Station! Where is it, then?"

"Not too long." He took her hand and started to walk. "Ganuchka, if you please, take off your so yellow bonnet."

"Bonnet? It isn't a bonnet, it's a – well, sort of cap."

"Take off, take off. You have beautiful hair."

"I know that line, it's *Uncle Vanya*!" She took off her hat, shook out her hair and twirled round. "Ellen did that scene with us – where Sonya says 'If a woman isn't beautiful, people always say, You have beautiful eyes, you have beautiful hair...'"

"You know our *Vanya*!"

"Only because Ellen forced it on us – 'You can't go to Russia without knowing Chekhov,' she said. We nearly murdered her by the end of Cherry blooming Orchard..."

"Ganuchka, I do not understand – 'force', 'murder' – this is not words for Chekhov..."

They were at the Metro station. Crowds of people were still milling about, chattering in cheerful huddles or wandering in family groups up and down the Prospekt. All down Prospekt Vernadskova the lights of Revolution Day were shining, red neon stars appearing and disappearing. Red flags fluttered against lamp-posts and red banners strained on their ropes in the wind. He turned, leaned towards her, and they kissed. It was the softest, sweetest, most natural kiss in the world.

When they drew apart, he smiled at her. She smiled back. She'd kissed him, and lived!

They joined the surge going down into the Metro, still holding hands and running a few paces whenever there was a gap in the crowd. She floated above the ground – a hovercraft.

It was hot down in the station compared with the biting wind outside, but she didn't feel hot with nerves like she'd done in the Arbat. She was drunk. I'm drunk with excitement, she thought, and maybe love. I don't really know him, but so what? I'm in the middle of Moscow, I don't know where we're going, and I'm taking the biggest risk I've ever taken – far bigger than going off to that rock concert with Phil without telling Mum and Dad. What's more, I'm not doing it just to show them, to drag their attention away from darling fragile Kate. I'm doing it simply because Kostya's wonderful, and I'm wonderful, and I'll remember this evening for the rest of my born days.

While they waited for the train she said, "I wonder if Jim will be at Nina's tonight. He's been ill. Well, hung over."

"Shim? Which boy calls Shim?" He held both her hands and stood close. He was just a little taller than she was.

"He's the one who... How on earth can I describe Jim?" Kostya switched on his mock-serious face again. "No, really, it was ghastly. He's so proper, so uptight" – she stood stiff as a caricature of the English public boy – "and he got drunk and nearly made love to a party apparatchik with the rest of us looking on."

"Poor Shim. I know this style boy. He is good but he is sad, so he takes vodka to make happy, then he is bad. Then – shame, he is shame."

Of course. Jim wasn't ill, he was ashamed. "You're right, Kostya – you're dead right." The train roared into the platform.

But the combination of cold wind and hot station was too much even for Abi's mum's cold remedies. She had to blow her nose. She found the wad of paper hankies in her pocket and took one out.

They stepped between the sliding doors, and a little slip of paper fluttered out of Mrs Haigh's wad of tissues on to the floor of the train. "What's that?" she said, snatching one of the high bars as the train started jerking. "It must be something of Abi's mum's."

Kostya bent swiftly down to pick it up. He grabbed a bar with his other hand, muttered to himself in Russian, then looked at her with shining eyes. "I know. I am certain sure. It is."

"What is it?"

"Come near." She did. In a low dark voice like something out of a John le Carré novel he murmured, "It is bedroom."

"What d'you mean?"

"This Abismum. She is sleeping in hotel?"

"Yes. No, just at the minute she's round at Nina's watching revolutionary TV."

"Is not possible for her to visit hotel room just now. This be – " he tickled her nose with the piece of paper – "Abismum's key."

"Key?"

They'd stopped at a station, and he spoke even lower. "Key paper. In hotel, persons cannot leave with key. They give key to *dezhurnaya*, who gives to them paper. On return – if wish to have key – " (the train began to move again) – "give paper to *dezhurnaya*, she gives key."

"But then – Abi's mum won't be able to get into her room!"

"*Nyet*." Kostya put the paper in his pocket. "But – we – are – able."

"Kostya!" His face swayed in front of her. Pulses on each side of her forehead began to throb. "But she'll come to her room!"

"She can not. No key. *Dezhurnaya* not allow into room without key. Safe, we be. For short time. Do not frighten, Ganuchka. I take care."

Megan looked down at her boots, then at Kostya's battered trainers – he must have got *those* on the black market – then at the swaying floor between.

"Ganuchka," he said again quietly. "Do not frighten. It be OK." His free hand took hers and he stroked the back of it with his thumb.

A bedroom, and Kostya. None of her fantasies had taken her that far. She wanted to put her face up for him to kiss there and then, but dared not look at his eyes.

The train stopped again. It was the end of the line. Kostya pulled her by the hand and they joined

153

the masses coming up out of the station. Out in the cold he stopped and kissed her again. She closed her eyes. Softness, sweetness.

Then he said, "Taxi." He ran over to a waiting car and some Russian magic of his – or did he have pounds or dollars in his pocket? – persuaded the driver to take them without argument. It was like fast-forward on the video. In a few minutes they were whisked to the courtyard that fronted the monstrous hotel.

Megan got out of the taxi. Her whole head was thumping now. Suddenly, panic set in. *Wait!* she wanted to shout. *It's too quick! I'm not ready!* What did Russian men expect? She might be no good at it! She'd wanted Dafydd to be first! And what had Mish said about contraception? Galoshes! What would she do with her contact lenses? – she couldn't leave them in, but she'd lose them if she took them out...

They were running up the hotel steps. Round a revolving door, and now they were faced with a uniformed man. Kostya waved the bit of paper at him and he nodded cheerfully. It was obviously a passport to this foreigners-only hotel. *Kostya – wait!* came the words inside Megan's head. And at the same time – *Kostya, yes!*

Across a lobby seething with people and suitcases, and on either side of a wide passageway stood people waiting for lifts. Kostya took a look at the key-paper. "*Vosyem,*" he said and chose one of the lifts. "Eight." When it came, six or eight people crowded in with them. He pulled her close as if they were a couple staying at the Salyut for their honeymoon, held her chin lightly and kissed her again.

During the kiss, her thoughts flashed like firework sparks. She could trust him, yes – but could she trust herself? Her mouth was saying *Yes!* – half her brain shouted *No! Slow down!* – the other half hoped against hope they'd get to the bedroom without a hitch and – oh yes, please! – that he'd thought about contraception –

The kiss ended. He let go of her and the lift stopped. "Seven," he said, without taking his eyes off hers. "One only more."

Eight. The doors slid open and they got out. There were no bedroom doors to be seen. There was a carpeted lobby with pot plants round the edges, a few easy chairs facing a flickering television on which Mr Gorbachev was chatting to reporters, and a desk. Behind the desk sat a large blonde woman with heavily made-up eyes, painting her fingernails.

Kostya led Megan over to the desk. Without a word he gave the blonde the magic paper. She took it casually and reached towards the rows of keys in pigeon-holes on her right. Kostya's hand tightened on Megan's.

The half-painted fingernails hovered over the pigeon-holes, then went into reverse gear and came to rest on the top of the desk. She held the magic ticket up for closer inspection. The mascara'd lashes flickered upwards, and she offered the ticket back to Kostya with a few lethargic Russian words.

Kostya, stepping even closer to Megan, said, "I so sorry. I speak not Russian. English please."

"Is woman," said the blonde, still lethargic. "Hair – " and the fingers drew in the air a spectacularly accurate sketch of Abi's mother's coiffure. "Man – " She pointed to the ceiling. Waving the ticket, she said, "*Klyooch* – key – not possible. *Nyevozmozhno.*" She held the ticket over the desk.

He snatched it rudely from the outstretched hand. Megan knew on the instant that he was about to blow it. He was going to reveal himself as a local by shouting in Russian. He'd be accused – evicted – arrested...

Sharply, in the alertness that sometimes precedes panic, she jerked his hand in hers.

"Maygann?" He was distracted and turned his face towards her, puzzled.

"Megan?" said Ellen's voice sharply behind them. "What are you doing here? Who's this?"

Megan shot round like a spinning top. "Ellen! It's – we've got – we found this ticket – " she whipped it from Kostya and held it out – "and thought we'd better..." She felt her face flush bright scarlet.

Ellen clicked her tongue. "It's here! We've been hunting high and low for that wretched... Mrs Haigh's downstairs, haranguing the management..." She stared hard at Kostya. "I'm sorry. Who are you? Didn't I see you the other night at the Arbat?"

"Kostya – our teacher, Miss Tudor-Williams. Ellen, this is Kostya, a friend of Riina's – he's an actor in the Students' Theatre..."

Ellen's lip tightened. She shook Kostya's hand.

"Delighted. I wondered why you weren't at Nina's flat, Megan, watching the Revolution Parades in Kiev and Tashkent. If you don't mind, er, Kostya –" and with a gulp she transferred to Russian, clearly saying it was time for him to leave. He argued only for a moment, in words that included "*Lysistrata*", to which Ellen answered, "*Da.*" Didn't that mean "yes"?

Kostya took Megan's hand and bowed to kiss it. "You will attend our play," he said. "I await. Until."

"Fine," said Megan as he walked away, still looking towards her. "OK." The lift arrived as if on cue. Two people got out and Kostya turned to step in. The doors closed before he had time to turn back and wave.

"Come and sit down, Megan," said Ellen. She walked towards the easy chairs. Megan had no option but to follow.

But Ellen didn't sit down. She stood with a row of pot plants behind her and faced Megan. Behind them, the television blared. "You always must have drama outside the theatre as well as in it, mustn't you, Megan?"

Megan stuttered, "There wasn't any problem – Kostya's trustworthy, kind, a sort of gentleman, like lots of Russians are..." Ellen was implying she'd gone with Kostya just to show off. How dare she!

"Gentleman! How do you know, Megan? How the hell can you *know*? Just what do you think was in that young man's mind, the moment before I arrived?"

"I – I don't know."

Ellen shook her head in despair. "You met him all of three days ago, and you were willing to come to this hotel for whatever purposes he dictated. With whatever diseases or pregnancies that might later ensue." Shut up – shut *up* – Kostya isn't, wouldn't, he'd look after me... Ellen leaned forward. "Megan, my duty is to get you back home on Friday intact, in every sense of the word."

God, would she tell Mum and Dad? She wouldn't! Why didn't she understand? If she was in love with Oleg, surely she'd understand!

She hardly heard what Ellen was saying. There was no need for her to be so contemptuous, so humiliating... But there was one sure thing. Ellen wouldn't let her go to *Lysistrata* tomorrow. She'd make sure she couldn't ever see Kostya again.

The clipped rebuke came to an end. "...given you credit for some degree of common sense, but it appears I was mistaken. I foolishly gave my permission for you to go to *Lysistrata* tomorrow," – Megan could hardly believe her ears – "because Riina asked me especially, and it would hardly be fair to forbid it now."

"Thanks, Ellen." Bless Riina. They could go.

"Though," Ellen went on, "you'll miss a trip to the Taganka Theatre if you do."

"The Taganka!" She knew how difficult it was to get tickets for the Taganka. Olwen said it was one of the best theatres in Moscow.

"Oleg managed to get tickets after all. But of course it's your duty to go to the Students' Theatre, isn't it?" She ran her fingers through her hair. It

158

seemed to Megan that she'd said yes to *Lysistrata* out of sheer exhaustion. She felt let down. Ellen had lost control.

"Now, I've got to get this key-ticket back to Mrs Haigh. And there are various other matters I've still got to sort out with Oleg before I get to bed. How the hell are you to get to Riina's flat? Megan, why did you have to...? I know. Mr Haigh's downstairs. He'll walk you home."

Megan got up. Her knees were itching to move. She was sick of being treated like an errant toddler. She wanted to run downstairs, and get to Riina's flat, and go to bed, and tomorrow to come.

But Ellen's weary voice refused to let her go. "Megan."

"Yes?"

"No more trouble. I've got enough on my plate with Jim and... Please. No – more – trouble. Promise?"

She'd never experienced so direct a plea. Ellen looked her in the eyes, then seemed ashamed of her pleading and looked beyond her towards the television.

A flicker of sympathy touched Megan. It must be Oleg. If love does this to you, she thought, maybe I'd better watch myself. "OK. I promise. Can I go now?"

CHAPTER NINE

Nowhere does time fly as it does in Russia.

Turgenev, *Fathers and Sons*

Mr Haigh merely nodded, of course, when asked to take Megan home. The two of them walked in silence round the revolving door out into the sharp night. Megan noticed that his nose was blue and he was wearing two pairs of gloves and two scarves. Poor Mr Haigh. No one took any notice of him, everyone used him as dogsbody, but actually he was suffering terribly from the cold.

Ellen had given permission for tomorrow. But they'd be in a crowded theatre. And then – what? "No – more – trouble." The cold cure had worn off and she was puffing and blowing into Mrs Haigh's tissues. When she went to *Lysistrata* tomorrow, she mustn't overdo the cold cure like this evening, she'd take two pills *or* two capsules...

"In my opinion," said Mr Haigh abruptly, blowing out a cloud of condensation and speaking to it rather than to her, "it was better when you knew where you stood."

"Oh?" said Megan politely. What was he talking about? She must be alone with Kostya somehow... Not go for it like they had this evening, but they must have a chance to say goodbye...

"East of Suez. Aden." (Wasn't it *East of Eden*?) "Uphold freedom wherever she's in danger. 'Poor little Poland,' my mother used to say. This Gorbcheff fellow, he seems like a gentleman, but you never can tell. Oh, you never can tell."

It was a speech! Megan wrenched her mind around and tried to connect with his. "You mean, if they were baddies and we were goodies, you can't believe they've turned into goodies now?"

"I remember my National Service number. Two-seven-six-four-three-four-one J.T. Haigh, J.M. I was one of the last."

One of the few? No, the Few were in the Second World War.

"'I vow to thee my country.' 'Final sacrifice.' National Service. I was in Malta. Wonderful sea. Sapphire blue. Nothing to do. Spent most of my time in the sapphire sea. And tomorrow, perhaps, a member of the Haydock household will answer the telephone."

Sea – Malta – Haydocks? Oh – Jim! "Was no one in at Jim's?"

"Mrs Garth Jones said not. Could you indicate...?"

"What? Oh, Riina's flat – it's the next block."

He seemed to fall back into the pit of his own silence. She wanted to ask him about Malta, but couldn't think of the right question... How could she be alone with Kostya again?

She and Mr Haigh went wordlessly up in the lift. She remembered being scared that her hair might tickle Mr Tormis' bald pate – light-years ago, last Wednesday night. Now her eyes were on a level with Abi's dad's two handknitted scarves, and she'd nearly been to bed with Kostya.

Outside Riina's flat he said, "That will be all, then," and made for the concrete stairs without even saying goodnight. Megan listened to him clattering down. As she rang the Tormises' bell, she realized that all these years she'd been holding it against the Haighs for taking over that house. For her it was always Dafydd's.

Riina opened the door. "Megan! You are alone?"

"Yes – Abi's father walked me from the … Kostya had to…"

Riina took her hand. "My parents are in their bed. You are tired? Hungry?"

"Hungry," said Megan, and they went into the kitchen.

Riina got out bread and jam. "I understand – Kostya must go to his home. Has he related to you, Megan, where is his home?"

"No, he hasn't let on a thing about himself. Riina – you're right. I do fancy him. Thanks a million for giving us time on our own."

Riina cut a large slice of malty bread in half, then into quarters. She seemed not to be thinking about what she was doing. "Why does he not bring you home? Why is it the duty of Mr Haigh?"

She mustn't tell Riina what happened. "Oh, we bumped into them and he…" Had Riina wanted Kostya to bring her home? Was that why she'd fixed it – so that he'd find out where she lived and,

when Megan had flown home, maybe come and…?
A convoluted way of getting a bloke interested in
you, but like Mr Haigh said, you never can tell.

But – tomorrow, in the group, Ellen might
mention her being at the hotel, Mrs Haigh might
say something about losing the key-ticket – she
might thank Megan for finding it. Surely Ellen
wouldn't let on to Abi's mother that Megan had
been alone with a strange Russian male? God!
Who was going to spill what beans to whom?
She'd have to tell Riina.

"I found this scrap of paper in my pocket," she
began and, between mouthfuls of bread and jam,
as gently as she could, she gave a summary of her
evening.

Then she looked up. Riina was staring away
from her, towards the window. The radio on the
window-sill was on and some crooning song
wafted out from it, very low. The song ended and
there was an electronic phrase from *Moscow
Nights*, like the pips coming on the hour at home.

"I don't think Kostya really meant —" Megan
began.

Riina put a finger to her lips. "Sssh – *Vremya*.
News." They both gazed firmly at the radio. "East
German things. Mr Krenz returns from Moscow to
Berlin. People flee from East Germany to West –
flee, flee, flee." She clicked the radio off. Megan
still couldn't see her face.

"Riina," she asked, "you told me Kostya said
things to you last week – about happiness and pain
or something. You hoped he might be interested in
you. Then I barged in, and he took a fancy to me.

163

What was it he said to you? Have I messed things up completely?"

Riina turned. Her small blue eyes had sunk farther into her head. "It is nothing. Likely I understood incorrectly. He told about a — what is it – partnership —"

"Relationship —"

"Relationship – most sad, most wounding to the heart – it is done, it is over for him. But —"

"But now, maybe he and you —?"

"He said that if she, the hurting one, would have been like me, he thinks no such wounds might be delivered. 'You are kind, Riina,' he says. 'You make a man happy.'"

"That's a lovely thing to say. And it's true, you will make someone happy."

"I am friend, Megan. Yes – kind, make happy. That is what friend does. But lover? No. Not me."

"But he's had a lover – this female who hurt him so much! Maybe he's having a final fling with me, then he'll turn to you and…"

"Believe that, Megan? Can you believe?"

"I don't know. Who can get inside men's minds? They're a total mystery to me. Riina – " Megan stared at the rest of jammy bread sitting uneaten on their plates. "What if Ellen hadn't come out of the lift at that moment? What if the *dezh*…"

"*Dezhurnaya*."

"…hadn't argued about the key? I was crazy – I might have gone home pregnant… Riina, stay beside me tomorrow, will you? I mustn't let myself in for that again."

* * *

On the way to the hotel next morning they met up with Mish and Nadya. When she glimpsed them in the distance, Megan's stomach plummeted. She'd been so tired and emotional when they went to bed that she'd forgotten to ask Riina what she'd told them about her disappearance.

Mish greeted them with, "Hi, Riina – hi, Meggo, who's the lucky one?"

"Erm —"

"How's the old cold? You missed some riveting telly. Twenty-five parades, one after another without stopping. Beats *Panorama* into a cocked hat, I can tell you."

"Me, I have longings for your *Panorama*," sighed Nadya.

"But Nadya," said Mish, leaning towards Riina and Megan confidentially, "tell these two what you suspect about that vodka the other night."

"*Nyet, nyet*, Nadya!" cried Riina, taking hold of her friend's arm and stopping her in her tracks.

"But why must I not, Riina?" Nadya pulled free and strode on. "If Oleg is in friendship with his Yelyena, the Pentre Corach must know of these things."

"What things?"

Ellen's exhaustion – *there are various matters I've got to sort out with Oleg.* Megan knew what Nadya was going to say before she said it.

"It is Oleg Stepanovich who has the ways of bringing vodka to our homes. It is he who was kind to Nina's party."

"Kind!" Riina burst out. "Vodka spoils – vodka makes ill – vodka makes bad…"

"Was it vodka that broke up his marriage?" asked Megan. "My friend Dafydd, his father was an alcoholic and —" She stopped. Would Riina assume she'd break with Dafydd now she'd been with Kostya? But she couldn't! And Dafydd's father *had* been alcoholic – she'd often seen him rolling out of pubs in Pentre. No wonder his mother hadn't come back there to live, till two years ago when his dad was killed at the wheel of his car.

"We have not the knowing about his marriage," said Nadya. "He says to us, 'Alcohol is bad for you.' But Vitya and Levan, you see how they wish manliness through vodka, how they make others also the same."

"Mish," Megan asked, "d'you reckon Oleg's in love with Ellen, then?"

"Of course! He loves!" cried Nadya. "Then he marries the British, he has permit for Britain. And then I get visa to Britain and visit they two!"

"It is in your mind only, Nadya," Riina argued. "True, Megan, we fear he has problem with the vodka. We love him, we give him respect. We know it is war between himself and the bottle, and we give to him our closest support. Vitya and Levan, it was bad of them to ask of him."

"Huh," grunted Nadya. "Levan, he respects not Oleg Stepanovich. But I ask myself," she said as they got near the hotel, "is Jim with us today?"

No, no sign of Jim. Dima said he'd eaten nothing. Nina looked depressed. Mrs Garth Jones was delegated to try again to get through to Jim's parents, while the rest took the coach to see the

Lenin Olympic Stadium and the open air swimming pool.

Abi marched over, pulled Megan away from Riina and sat beside her in the coach. "What have I done, then, Shipway?" she demanded.

"Done?" How could Abi know about Kostya if Mish didn't?

"If you were planning to lose yourself in Moscow you might have taken me along, you rat. Mum said you got back here and she forced old Dad to see you safely home!"

"I – I jumped into a taxi and..." Relief.

"I'm marginally pissed off with you, as a matter of fact. Abandoned to the mercies of dear Nina, who's in floods of tears over her darling Jim... You've always got to be different, haven't you?" Not for the first time, Megan could imagine Abi turning out like her mother. "Off to the Students' Theatre – special dispensations... Ellen's losing her touch, in my opinion. She should stop getting at Oleg. See how she needles him? 'Course he's not a flipping saint, brilliant directors never are."

"Brilliant? How come he's not directing at the Taganka or the Moscow Arts, then?"

"Nina says it was his marriage. When they bust up, his wife got off with another director and made sure Oleg got sweet nowhere."

"Oh! No wonder he hit the bottle."

"He didn't 'hit the bottle'! Men've got to have some fun, haven't they? Like Jim – I told Nina – it's just his sheltered life, he needed to have some fun."

A penny dropped in Megan's brain. "You're not getting some kind of crush on old Oleg, are you,

Abi?" It wasn't too far-fetched. With a dad like hers, Abi might just fall for a father figure.

"Don't be daft, he's *ancient*!" Abi was blushing.

Megan was sure she'd struck a nail neatly on the head. But she wanted peace and quiet to think what was going to happen tonight. She said, "I don't think Jim's ill, I think he's embarrassed. Ashamed."

"He'll get over it," said Abi, her blush receding. "And you're off to this Greek stuff, are you? Rather you than me, mate. And if you fancy this actor creature and he's not interested, don't come crying to *me* for comfort."

"Anyone for going in?" asked Tie as the coach parked beside the open air swimming pool. "Not bloody likely, as the poet said," was the general response. They got out and looked at the clouds of steam and the heads of stout Muscovites pounding up and down. "It is heated throughout the winter," announced Sylvia. "At air temperature of many degrees below zero, people still swim here."

It was a bright, chill day. They'd found the Olympic Stadium less than fascinating, packaged as it was with lectures on the West's boycott of the 1980 Olympic Games when the Soviet Union invaded Afghanistan, and Soviet virtue in pulling out of Afghanistan again. Riina asked Megan innocently, "Will the English perhaps withdraw themselves from Wales one day?"

"Me, get out of Wales?" Megan was indignant.

"Oh," smiled Riina, "I forgot that you are belonging to the invading force." She was calm and balanced again. How could she separate the different parts of herself like this? Was she planning to stick by Megan tonight, or what?

On the way back, they crossed the bridge and drove along beside the river. Ellen pointed out an elegant building set back from the road, behind trees and high wrought-iron railings. "The British Embassy," she said. "Any passport problems, visas, personal crises – knock on their door. It's your piece of British property in the middle of Moscow."

"There go I," said Nadya confidently, "when I get visa for London. One day I will, surely!"

"But you're all coming over to us next year, aren't you?" said Mish.

"Of course, of course," said Nadya. "If currency allow it."

Back to the Salyut Hotel for their lunch where, after cold meats with beetroot, they had Russian ice-cream, which even Abi agreed tasted delicious. "What now, Ellen?" they asked.

"Now – shopping." Ooohs and aaahs from the girls, groans from the boys. "There's a good hard currency shop in the hotel," she said firmly. "Your loving families will be dying to see what presents you've got for them. And we'll be doing the economy a favour if we spend masses of pounds sterling. Am I being tactless, Oleg?"

"Realistic, my dear Yelyena."

"Be quick in the Beriozhka shop, then off to the studio for last minute rehearsals." She turned to Mrs Garth Jones, who'd just made another attempt to phone the Haydocks. "The cleaner? Isn't that just...! What more can we do?"

Abi said, "Well, I think Nina should go and see him."

After an embarrassed ripple round the group, there came a chorus of "What about it, then, Nina?"

Scarlet spread over Nina's broad face. "A privilege – if I could give service..."

"All right," said Ellen. "Oleg, can Nina be excused rehearsals? Fine. The rest – in the lobby, three o'clock."

All was mutterings and shufflings in the studio. Spock got busy with screwdriver and plugs to set up the keyboard, Mari gave sporadic twangs on the guitar and Tie on bass, while the rest hummed snatches of *West Side Story* and phrases from *Carousel*. In the opposite corner the Moscow group had their heads together in intense consultation with Oleg.

At long last Spock put his screwdriver away and Ellen shifted them into lines for "America". "Are we disturbing your concentration?" she called. But Oleg was deep in argument with Levan and didn't reply.

In rehearsal, Megan forgot about her cold, Riina, *Lysistrata*, even Kostya and Dafydd. As Anita she'd got the best lines in "America", and she gave them all she'd got. She flung her legs out, threw her hair around dramatically and, bated by Ellen – "More, more! Show me!" – responded to all the Puerto Rican enthusiasm about America with just the right cynical scorn.

Then Bryn Corach took centre stage to lead

170

"When You Walk Through a Storm". The Pentre six had enough Welsh to sing in the right language, and one sharp look from Ellen stopped them hamming it up as if they were on the Kop at Anfield.

Now Megan's contact lenses began to sting. Was it real emotion, or was this cold going to ruin her eyes? Might she have to take her lenses out and be half-blind for her last two precious days in Moscow?

The last phrase died away. They looked round. How had Oleg's lot been doing, with this racket going on?

They'd disappeared. But, as the electronic zing of the keyboard faded, a figure walked backwards through the far doorway. It was Nadya.

Step by step she walked, in terror. Step by step after her came Levan, holding aloft a large pillow. As he put each foot forward, he hissed out fury in tiny staccato bursts. The pair moved in jerks to the centre of the room, followed by the rest of the group – a silent, stealthy, magnetized audience.

Pentre Corach couldn't understand Levan's words, but the sense was crystal clear. Nadya was innocent, and she had to die.

Megan moved closer to Mish. There was an absolute seriousness in what the Moscow lot were doing that made their songs look frivolous.

Nadya was kneeling now. She couldn't escape Levan. He raised the pillow and brought it slowly down towards her face. She leant farther back – the pillow followed, a step away. She collapsed, and thud! – down went the pillow. He was smothering her.

Mish nudged Megan. "*Othello*!" she mouthed. Of course. Othello and Desdemona. Power turned to madness. Then Megan nudged Mish. Out of the corner of her eye she'd noticed someone standing by the main doors.

It was Abi. Megan hadn't realized she'd been absent from the rehearsal. She was trying to attract their attention.

Desdemona sank into oblivion and Othello stood triumphant. Abi beckoned, and Megan ran over on tiptoe.

"Now who's been losing herself in Moscow? Where've you been?"

"With Nina to see Jim," whispered Abi. "He's here!"

"Jim?"

Abi nodded. "We convinced him he hadn't done – well, anything. He couldn't remember a thing!"

"Ssssh," whispered Megan. The two groups had got into a circle to discuss the meaning of *Othello*. "But why don't they just come straight in?"

"Face, is my opinion. Losing it. Jim can't bear to."

"What if we sang? Could he slither in at the back?"

"I'll ask." Abi disappeared, and came back in a moment, nodding.

"'Walk Through a Storm?'"

Abi nodded again.

Megan ran over, waited for a pause in the

discussion, then cleared her throat. She said, "Sorry, but can we do our song over again, so that Jim can join in?"

Surprise flashed round every face. Then Oleg said, "Of course!" In two minutes Pentre Corach were set up again, backs to the door and with Spock at the keyboard. Between "At the end – of the storm – is a gold-en sky" and "sweet – silver song – of a lark" Jim slipped into place at the back. No one turned, and Jim sang along with the rest. Then Nina glided across the floor and joined the Moscow gang in applause.

The Students' Theatre was packed. Megan felt comfortable among the audience flowing in through the big shabby doors. They were mostly about her age, chattering in huddles or calling up and down the stairs as if they felt at home. They didn't expect to see Yuri and Kostya till after the performance, they'd be busy getting into costume and make-up backstage.

Mish had decided she couldn't bear to miss a visit to the Taganka, and Nadya agreed. "Yuri will be disappoint, Nadya," said Riina. "Let him disappoint," retorted Nadya.

"Stick by me, won't you, Riina." Riina nodded, too brightly. Megan felt guilty and confused. She must be careful of theatrical euphoria. She'd fallen for Phil when he'd gate-crashed the *Bugsy Malone* party.

They sat near the middle, close enough to see but far enough away from the stage. The play was late starting and the audience began a slow handclap. Then the Master of Ceremonies appeared, tall and thin as Spock, with a mobile face and total comic confidence. He waited till every giggle had died away, and announced in English: "Ladiezzz and Gennelmen – *Lysistrata*! Or... You Can't Get It Big Every Day!"

That slickness set the tone. Megan's attention was caught from start to finish, though every line but the first was in Russian. She felt a bit breathless when Kostya came on stage, but managed to save her nose-blowing for the interval.

Kostya was completely absorbed in the action. Even when he, a warring husband, had to watch his wife ballet-dance her withdrawal of favours, he kept all eye-contact for the stage. How could she have thought otherwise? And he could act – he was relaxed, witty, and an excellent acrobat. Yuri was chief husband and had a larger part. He used his angular eyebrows to good effect, but Megan felt he was too serious for a comedy like this.

During the interval she glimpsed Uncle Vanya sitting on the front row, arms crossed tight, chin thrust down. "He's *exactly* like an orang-utan!" she said to Riina in the lobby. "Orang? Oran-ge?" Megan was feeling light-headed again and she growled and loped around like an anthropoid ape. At last Riina laughed, but tensely.

By the end of the play, the men had stopped fighting and the women kissed them – the classic happy ending. But the MC raised a hand to quell the applause. He caught hold of Kostya and pulled him downstage. In Russian, but with gestures that anyone could understand, he said to Kostya, "All this – the play, the jokes, the dancing – what does it really mean, to these people out here?"

Megan's heart drummed. Kostya – cat's eyes – soft kisses... "It means," said Kostya to the audience, and her, "that the most important thing in the world is peace."

He turned to the audience and spread out his arms. In Russian, Greek and English he repeated: "*Mir – Eirene – Peace.*"

There was a hushed pause, then the audience broke into ecstatic applause. Megan blew her nose and so, beside her, did Riina.

They walked among the crowds out on to the chandeliered landing, and a wave of exhaustion engulfed Megan.

They'd bought bottles of Pepsi and little bars of Russian chocolate from the hotel shop to share with Kostya and Yuri after the show, but all she wanted to do was go home, take out her itching lenses and fall into bed. Kostya was wonderful – inspiring – she was still swallowing back tears over that peace bit – but Ellen was right, she hardly knew him. She must leave him to Riina.

The crowds thinned out as people disappeared down the stairs. "They will not have too much time for us." Riina sat down cross-legged. "They must do their part in breaking down the set."

"Riina, you're so calm!"

Riina gave a wry smile. "I am friend, not lover." She took a bottle-opener from her pocket and opened two Pepsis. "You are not calm?"

"I'm —" Megan took a Pepsi and sipped it – "I'm fizzy in the head."

Riina addressed her formally. "What is your opinion, Megan, of our actors' skill? Are Moscow student actors as clever as your British?"

"Oh, cleverer," replied Megan, playing her part. "You are so disciplined. You can sing, dance, and to top it all you're comedians as well." She glanced at the doorway for signs of Yuri and Kostya. "But that *Othello* stuff isn't exactly stand-up comedy, is it?"

"Of course it is no comedy." Riina turned huffy. "One does not laugh at life's tragedies."

"But why did you choose it? If it had to be Shakespeare, couldn't you do, oh, *Midsummer Night's Dream*?"

"But Megan – the large questions of our life, they are all serious." And Riina was serious now. "Which man has power, which man suffers, how to be true and good."

Those are the large questions of your life, are they? thought Megan. Mine are: what job I'm going for – which male I'll settle down with, and when – whether to go for money or happiness, or try and get both. Are you really concerned about the Meaning of Life, Riina, when we're going to face Kostya in a few seconds' time?

"We have made the play of *Othello* into our own play," said Riina. "The man Othello, he is this Soviet state. He loves his little wife, his people – he loves her so much that he must stop all breath from her."

"Don't be so serious all the time! What about

176

films, videos, rock music? You'd get like Nina, droning on about the needs of the nation, if you didn't have a bit of fun!" Now she sounded mindlessly non-political. Riina was too old for sixteen – Megan couldn't keep up. "Riina," she said urgently, "when Kostya comes, I want you to..."

"Take Yuri, and leave two alone? No?"

"No. I don't know." She plonked her Pepsi down, and some froth bubbled over and trickled on to the carpet. "I don't know anything. I'm absolutely knackered."

She watched Riina scribbling *knackered* in her notebook, then looked up. Kostya and Yuri were walking towards them.

Her insides did a somersault. I will resist him, she thought, I will.

Yuri's face fell. No Nadya. "*Isvinitye,*" he grunted. "Excuse – moment," and ran downstairs two at a time.

Kostya sank down cross-legged beside the girls. "Cigarette, Yuri needs. And his Nadya." He put out his hands to take theirs. Megan pretended she thought he meant to shake hands and quickly withdrew hers. Riina held on for a moment longer.

His cat-like eyes flashed. "We are good, yes? Ganuchka? We are great, marvellous, most completely tremendous?"

Megan tried to be casual. She passed him a bar of chocolate. "You were terrific. But is tonight the only performance? What a waste!"

"Waste? Rub-bish? You think we be rub-bish?" He waved the chocolate wrapper.

"No – I didn't mean... It's a pity more people

can't see it." He was angry, she didn't want him to be angry. "I nearly cried when you said that at the end. About peace."

Kostya gave her his grave look – mocking, or real? "But it is true. You do not think?"

"I've never thought about it. I mean, there's never been a war in my whole lifetime – hardly in my parents' even."

"You West. No wars on your land, no Stalin. You do not know. Lucky, lucky."

"Lucky who?" Yuri bounded up the stairs again. He swung round the banister and crouched down.

"People of West, Yuri. Agree?"

"Sure, I agree." Yuri gave a sour grin and stretched his hands, knuckles cracking as usual. "West, all is perfect good. But! Tough is the life, the true life. Tough is Russia, where I live." Megan, relaxing at last, caught Riina's eye at 'Russia'. "Is Russia that I live *for*."

"Ah, Russia, she is old, tired, worn away," said Kostya. "West is young. Is so, yes, Ganuchka? Rock, pop, laugh! We need!"

"Pep-si Co-la!" scorned Yuri. He took a swig and wiped his mouth. "Hamburgers! Fishanchips! West has all!"

"Compact discs," said Megan defensively. "Motorways. The National Health. Democracy – votes every five years – "

"I have heard this." Yuri pushed aside Riina's offer of chocolate. "I have speaked with many British on this. You – " He thrust his head at Megan. "You have Member of Parliament? Yes?"

178

"Of course I do."

"The name?"

"What d'you mean, name?"

"Of your Parliament member?"

"Um…"

"Is so! See! You have great democracy, in which the people are ignorant even of the fact!"

Megan flushed, furious. She did know the man's name – it was…

Kostya laughed. He took her hand again. "Ganuchka, this night you will awake with the name. Is always so." She gave him a forced smile and tugged at her hand. But he hung on.

A moment's silence, broken by Riina. "Yuri, Nadya sends many sorrows. She must be tonight at theatre with Oleg Stepanovich."

"Must be, must be." Yuri's fingers hovered. He was dying for another cigarette.

"Don't worry, Yuri! Be happy!" said Kostya. "Is not possible to love an angry man!"

"I wish happiness of realness, I do not wish happiness of illusion," Yuri declared, drawing out his syllables contemptuously.

"I also, I also." Kostya gave Megan a puzzled look – she'd managed to retrieve her hand. He turned to Riina. "Riina, you give Maygann a most happy time?"

"Megan? You have most happy time?"

"Fantastic, amazing," replied Megan. She couldn't keep the weariness out of her voice.

"Ganuchka – you sad, you worry, you fear?"

"No. I'm just dead beat." She didn't have to explain.

Riina got up and helped Megan to her feet. Now she'd got pins and needles. Head, tummy, feet, all were fizzy as Pepsi. "We must go," said Riina.

"But – when you leave?" asked Kostya, putting a hand on Megan's shoulder. "Leave Moscow – go London?"

"Friday. Tenth. Day after tomorrow."

"Tomorrow." He turned her round and spoke earnestly. "We meet. Where?"

Megan looked at Riina. She had to meet him – but she couldn't, mustn't. In any case, how?

Riina said, her hair falling over her face, "Megan, Oleg Stepanovich tells us we take our friends to centre Moscow tomorrow. Morning, our performances. Evening, a slight banquet. Afternoon, to see sights for last time."

"Red Square," said Kostya. "By Vladimir Ilyich Lenin. Two – three?"

"Three," said Megan. Riina would arrange it. Ellen would never know. She couldn't not say goodbye.

"OK. Until."

"*Pakka*." She was amazed at herself for bringing out the right word.

CHAPTER TEN

Like the wives of Peter's troopers in Red Square,
I'll stand and howl under the Kremlin towers.

Anna Akhmatova, *Requiem*

She couldn't sleep. Her cold decided it had been fended off long enough; it was going to force its way through the cure barrier. She was shivering. It'd be just her luck to get flu. She turned over.

"You are awake, Megan?" breathed Riina in the darkness.

"Yes. Are you?" They whispered a laugh.

"You scare about Kostya?"

"Yes. Is there any way I can make it right for you?"

"Not possible. It is for Kostya to do." Riina sniffed, and Megan knew it wasn't a cold. "I like your Ellen, Megan. She is strong person, she can live alone. She has not married?"

"No. Far as I know, she's completely on her own. She's got parents in Merthyr or Cardiff or somewhere, but I think they're divorced. D'you think she's in love with Oleg?"

"All, we all are in love with Oleg Stepanovich. No – he is our father, our special father."

"And he drinks."

181

"Megan – " Riina said it almost like "Maygann" – "you may make it right for me, perhaps."

"With Kostya?"

"You may tell to him my address here. Now it is Students' Theatre no longer – is no more rehearsing, performing, not until the next year. So I may not see him, unless... Say, if he wishes news of you, to come and see. I will be friends to him, I can be a friend. Lover is not necessary."

Megan stretched a hand over to the other bed, and Riina took it. "Then you'll get close, and your love will be real, not just infatuation, and he'll say, How can I manage without you, and when your folks go back to Estonia you'll stay behind with him – "

"No! Is not possible!" Riina gulped and went back to a whisper. "You cannot understand this Moscow. One cannot stay in Moscow. One needs permit to allow. We Tormises have permit because they need my father. But without – no. And I will go home. Tallinn – she is always my home." She gave Megan's hand a squeeze and blew her nose. "We sleep, Megan. Tomorrow is busy day."

"*Nos da*, Riina."

"Pardon?"

"It's 'good night' in Welsh."

"Ah! *Head ööd*, Megan."

"Estonian?"

"Yes. Sleep very well."

Megan closed her eyes. She fought to keep Kostya out of her head. She made herself think about soap – the pack of three tablets that Mum had stuffed in her suitcase saying they'd been a present from Uncle Norman and Auntie Peggy, she couldn't stand lavender and maybe Riina's mum might like to have them. The Tormises had spread them round the house as if there wasn't another bar of soap in the USSR. One was in the bathroom, one in the kitchen, and Riina had put the third in her drawer to breathe English lavender through her smalls.

Mustn't think about Kostya. Think about going home. "Thanks," she'd said, to calm Mum's anxiety, "but Dafydd says he'll wait for the coach. Can we give you a ring from the call-box in Stryd Fawr when we're ready to be picked up?" Megan and Dafydd – Dafydd and Megan. That's how it was. Then how could she fall for Kostya?

Kostya was – how old? Eighteen? He'd probably had dozens of girlfriends. Slept with them. He was romantic – he'd pick them up and drop them. One night stands? Did they have Aids in Moscow? What should she tell Dafydd? How could she fancy Kostya if she fancied Dafydd? It was different – there was no comparison!

But who'd believe that? Would Dafydd? When she finally fell asleep she dreamt about a little face peering round a heavy green village hall door.

They were late at the studio. Over breakfast Mrs Tormis had got eloquent about Baltic fish recipes and they hadn't the heart to stop her.

Oleg was in the far corner lambasting Levan. Nadya, wearing Mish's enormous *Save the Rainforests* sweatshirt, sat applying eye make-up and awaiting her cue. Nina and Jim stood hand in

183

hand as if there were no tomorrow. Abi hovered nearby.

Ellen, in the opposite corner, was trying to stop Tom and Llyr belting out "Tonight – *Nos da*" while smothering Olwen as if she was Othello's Desdemona. She took no notice of Megan's arrival. Sharply, she called them to order. "The Moscow group will present their piece first. Then we'll do 'America' and the 'Tonight' sequence, and conclude with *Carousel*. Quiet!" She put up an irritated hand to Spock and Mari on keyboard and guitar. "Othello is preparing for curtain up."

They all knew Ellen was a reformed smoker, and for the first time Megan noticed her right hand drawn towards her mouth. Oleg was now eyeball to eyeball with Levan.

"Come on, let's get going," whispered Mish. "Nadya's tense enough already without all this hassle."

Megan decided to confide in Mish. "Mish, d'you know what the rules are for this afternoon?"

"Coach to the Arbat, apparently, then DIY tourism for a couple of hours." She looked squarely at Megan. "Why, what are you plotting? Meggo – what's it with Yuri's friend? How was the play?"

"Great. Yuri was mad that Nadya wasn't there. How was Taganka?"

"Brilliant. And was Kostya thrilled to see you? What's the score?"

"I'm to be at Lenin's Mausoleum at three. And my head's splitting in half, and my sinuses are filled up with lead."

"Which reminds me. Abi's mum said to give you this." She fished in her canvas bag and brought out a mini-inhaler.

"Well! I never thought I'd call that old bag an angel!"

"Meggo..." Mish held the plastic bottle away from her grasp. "Your date with Lenin. Is Riina going to be around? Or Yuri?"

"No one."

"Happy?"

"Yes. Terrified."

"What about Dafydd?"

"I don't know. But I can't miss this, not for anything."

Mish handed over the bottle. "Go steady, girl. What about Ellen?"

They both turned. Ellen was sitting on her own, fingers in arrested motion half-way through her hair, staring into space. "I think Ellen's got problems of her own," said Megan.

Nadya's Desdemona brought Pentre Corach to their feet. She was dignified, courageous and defiant. Mish rushed over to give her a hug and tell her to keep the rainforest sweatshirt as a souvenir.

Megan had given her nose a couple of squirts with the inhaler and felt better. Ellen started to arrange Pentre Corach in lines for their songs. But Oleg stopped her.

"Wait, Yelyena! *Othello* is Shakespeare's play, England's – Britain's play. You must play it, you Britskis."

"Very well," said Ellen. "Who'll have a go? Tie,

185

Meredydd, like to play Othello?" Meredydd and Tie looked horrified. The other lads dissolved into the shadows.

Oleg smiled. "It makes them shy," he said. "Right. First I am Othello – " he took the pillow from Levan – "with a Britski Desdemona. Then Ellen is Desdemona to your Britski Othello."

"Just actions," said Ellen. "We don't all know the words."

"Go on, Meggo," urged Mish. "You'd make a fantastic Desdemona."

"Not on your life. Abi, you do it!" She knew Abi – Abi wouldn't do it.

"I'll try," said Abi. She walked over to Oleg and followed him till they were nearly off-stage.

Suddenly he turned, raising the pillow. The lines on his face, in the dim studio light, looked like scars.

"'Put out the light – '" The words came out like stabs.

Abi stepped back in terror. Megan was taken aback – Abi could act! Oleg threatened her, step by obsessive step. "'And then…'" stab – stab – "'put out the light.'" Or – was the terror real?

"'When I have pluck'd the rose – '" Oleg lifted the pillow high – "'I cannot give it vital growth again…'"

Abi screamed.

"Abigail!" called Ellen. "There's no scream – just mime – " She was half-way through the word "mime" when everyone saw that Abi was crying.

Ellen ran across the floor and, arms round Abi and murmuring soothing words, she drew her to a side doorway. Megan glanced at Mish. "I'd better go," she mouthed. She ran over. Ellen had her arm round Abi, who was heaving with sobs.

Ellen eased Abi over to Megan. "Thanks, Megan. Sorry, Abigail. I've got to have words with Oleg." She paused for a second, breathed in and went back through the door.

Megan was stumped. Abi never cried. What should she say? Sorry for abandoning her to Nina? For finding romance in Moscow – if Abi knew anything about that?

No, this was about Oleg. But she mustn't say so. "What you need is a fag," she said. "Have you got one handy?"

"Can't smoke inside," Abi sniffed.

"Come on out, then."

"Fags're in there – " jerking her head at the main studio. "'S'all right. Stop coddling. Take a squint and say when they're lining up. I'm going to sing."

Megan went and squinted. Ellen and Oleg were arranging the crowd for Pentre Corach's presentation. She came back, lent Abi a tissue to wipe her face, and they went in.

Megan's performance as Anita went so brilliantly that she thought she might try for RADA after all. Abi pretended nothing had happened. I wish my face recovered that quickly from crying, thought Megan. Ellen sat in the shadows at the edge of the room. Oleg had disappeared.

During the "Tonight" sequence, when she was only in the chorus, Megan's concentration lapsed.

Kostya! The song might have been invented specially for them, for today. *To-night – to-night...* "This afternoon – this afternoon" didn't sound so romantic and it didn't scan, but for Megan it might have been Shakespearean poetry.

The applause for *West Side Story* was wild enough for a first night at the Moscow Arts. Then came *Carousel*. They lined up for "When You Walk Through a Storm", Spock gave them a chord, and they began.

"Hold your head – up – high – " She saw Jim's eyes fixed on Nina. Had Gentleman Jim found true love at last, then? Hey – what if Abi was holding a secret candle for *Jim*?

"And don't – be afraid – of the dark," she sang, and caught Riina's eye. She mustn't be so spellbound by Kostya that she forgot to give him Riina's address.

She glimpsed the small shy figure of Sasha. He was kneeling on the studio floor, eyes bright and hands poised to clap furiously the minute they'd finished the song. Levan, arrogant Levan – even he was caught up in it. As they sang the last line, he ran over to Spock at the keyboard. Megan heard him whisper, "Again – and say to us the English words!"

Spock got the message. He started up again and as each line finished, he shouted out the next one. The groups sang together in a mixture of Welsh, English and Russian, "Walk on – walk on – with hope – in your heart – And you'll ne-ver – walk – a-lone..."

Megan saw Oleg creep in at the back. He edged

188

his way round the side of the room and stood by the keyboard. When he got there he put out a hand towards Ellen in the shadows. Would she come to him? Her face was turned away. But then her eyes seemed to be dragged round. She looked at him, shrugged her shoulders as if to say *Must I?* then walked quietly over.

Along the line of singers from Megan was Abi, eyes brimming with tears and chin creased to stop it trembling. Oleg, who was clutching Ellen's hand to his scruffy sweater, started singing too. Megan thought the battered building would burst. She sang till her lungs hurt. We were two groups, she thought, and we've fused into one – a rich fruity Christmas pudding of warm togetherness. I can't believe that in three and a half hours' time I'll be alone with Kostya.

"You are certain of your way?" Riina asked, when they'd thrown off the others by nipping up an alleyway off the Arbat.

"Certain." Megan patted her shoulder-bag with the map, wodges of paper tissues, and the last of the chocolate bars to share with Kostya. "I'll give him your address and tell him you're wonderful."

"No! OK, Megan – yes. I hope that you will have a good afternoon!"

"And you."

Riina grimaced. All she was doing was queuing at a *gastronom* for her mother. Megan leaned forward to give her cheek a grateful peck, and Riina gave her three pecks, Russian-style. "Five-thirty, Metro Arbatskaya."

189

The sun shone. Approaching the Kremlin from Kalinin Prospekt, following her map carefully, she came up the hill into Red Square at the opposite end from St Basil's and got a glimpse of the gold onions of the cathedrals glowing in sunshine for the first time.

The cold bit her cheeks, but the sight of the sun kidded her that it was almost warm. She felt calm. She'd decided how to play her time with Kostya. She'd be cool. She'd talk an hour or so with him, exchange addresses and give him Riina's. Riina would win him, after she'd gone. Today, they'd kiss – wonderful. But it wouldn't go any further. There was nowhere they could go to be private, no time to declare undying love. She took off her gloves and hat, stuffed them into her bag, and shook her hair over her shoulders.

The queue to see Lenin still stretched right down to the Tomb of the Unknown Soldier, and crowds milled around in Red Square. The two main days of the Revolution holiday were over, but families seemed to be enjoying the last bit of break together before the routine of nursery, school and factory started again.

It was a couple of minutes before three. She saw Kostya, his coat unbuttoned and his shirt open at the neck, standing to one side of the Mausoleum queue with his hands in his pockets. She came and stood beside him, and he put out a hand.

Two grey-coated, high-booted guards approached in goose-step, bayonets balanced on white gloves. As the clock on the Saviour's Tower struck three they carried out their precise guard-changing routine under the massive marble lettering of L E N I N. Then once again the queue began to move.

"Ganuchka," said Kostya, turning and taking her other hand. "Kostya," she replied. She'd forgotten how his cheeks creased into long happy lines when he smiled. But she hadn't forgotten his cat-like eyes.

He didn't put his arms round her, but leaned and kissed her over the space between them. She felt safe. Only Lenin and a few thousand others were watching them. They had a couple of hours in front of them and the whole of Moscow was their playground. Wales, home and Dafydd settled into a quiet walled space in her mind and contented themselves with giving this tiny patch of ground to a Russian stranger.

He took her bag and put it over his own shoulder. "The play night," he said as they walked towards the grubbily striped knobs of St Basil's. "The night last…"

"Last night?"

"You feared. You angry. Which?"

"Feared. I'm not used to making assignations in foreign capitals – arranging to meet strange men…"

"Strange? Not! Be I strange to you, Ganuchka?"

She laughed. "No."

"Then – I make you happy. Show you Moscow. Where? Inside Kremlin? – you been. The bell who never can ring … the cannon who can never fire…"

"The icons that can never be kissed…"

"You are my icon," said Kostya, and kissed her again.

He decided they'd try to get into St Basil's and he'd show her the weaponry of Ivan the Terrible. But the man on duty was on his coffee break and the door was locked. So they went down behind the concrete Rossiya Hotel ("Tourism," said Kostya, "she is more terrible than Ivan.") in search of a tiny five-domed church hidden almost underneath the road. "Near to here," he said, "lived once a holy icon, Mother Virgin, and her kisses did give to every people…" Not knowing the word, he broke into melodramatic gestures of heaving and vile skin eruptions. "The plague?" asked Megan. "Ugh!"

"Was your *babushka* a holy woman?" she asked, as they came out of the gloomy church into the eye-hurting sunshine.

"Holy indeed, yes. I – not holy, not one bit. But I go church, I light candle for her."

He stopped at the bottom of the steps. "I have gift for you, Ganuchka. Small gift, but for you."

"Gift? But I've got nothing to give you!"

"The gift from you – is you." He put his hand in his pocket and took out a tiny newspaper parcel.

It was the smallest icon imaginable, painted in red, black and gold, and framed in cheap gilt. "He is Saint Nicholas. You say, I think, Santa Claus? He loves us young, my *babushka* did say. He loves you and me. He takes care for you, when you are flown."

"Thank you – thank you, Kostya. It's beautiful. I'll treasure it always." She put her face up for a kiss. A thought floated across her mind – *I don't care what happens now. This is a perfect moment.*

Another thought floated from the opposite direction – *I couldn't show the icon to Mum and Dad and Kate, they'd say it's shabby and crude. But I could show it to Dafydd.*

She gave it back to him to put in her bag, and they went up the steps to the street. "When did she die, your *babushka*?" she asked.

"Two year ago. I were – *syemnadtsat*... seventeen." So he was nineteen. Not that much older than her.

"I don't see much of my grandparents," she said. "They live in London. Did you go back to live with your parents then?"

"Parents? They be not parents to me. Parents love the children!"

"And yours didn't?"

"Huh!" said Kostya, and took her hand to run down towards the river.

Along the road between the Kremlin Wall and the Moskva River, they punctuated their walk by stopping for kisses and leaning on the wall. The leafless trees looked down at them and the cars and Intourist coaches rushed by.

They watched the brown shining water and talked. "You love the play? You go much to the Shakespeare, the Stratford?" Yes, she'd been to Stratford when they'd taken a holiday cottage in the Cotswolds, and twice with Ellen on trips from Pentre. "You become National actress, play as Glenda Jackson, Judi Dench?" Never! She'd probably do English and History A-levels and then, who knew. "What is 'a levels', Ganuchka?"

She asked, "What about you, Kostya? You're studying law, but drama's really your passion, isn't it?" She wanted to know about him, just like she wanted to know about Dafydd and his parents. Not so much the facts, more how he felt, what it was like having parents who were useless and grandparents you loved. But no, Kostya said. "Me? I have not interest in me. We talk of you, Ganuchka, of you."

When they reached the next bridge, he said, "Up to Bolshoi Kammenyi Most."

"Bolshoi? Like the ballet?"

He laughed. "*Bolshoi?* It mean big, great. Now. I show you good and bad Moscow, in one. New and old Moscow. Moscow of Tsar, and Moscow of Lenin, Stalin."

Up on Great Kammenyi Bridge, Megan could see what he meant. On the right, a heavily decorated iron parapet, and over it the red Kremlin towers, elegant façades and glistening cathedrals. On the left, tram-wires and squat faceless buildings, tedious tower-blocks and tatty offices.

"Over there in the distance – isn't that the University?"

"No, Ganuchka, that is hotel. Our friendly enemy, Josef Stalin, builded seven the same. This bridge, she is the first bridge across the —"

"Ouch!" Megan shot her hand up to her face, her left eye, in sudden agony.

"Ganuchka! Tell me what is!"

"No – it's OK – it's only – "

"What is? Ganuchka…" Gently he tried to pull her hand away.

194

"God! A bit of grit – it must have got underneath!"

"In eye? Take hand away, Ganuchka. I will see – "

If he tried to poke her lens out, it'd shoot out on to the pavement – or dig itself into her eye… "No," she gasped. "Leave it – my eyes'll water, it'll come out of its own accord…" Already her eye was full of tears. The pain was excruciating.

"I will, Ganuchka – allow, please…"

"No! It's my lens, it's happened before, just wait – "

"Lens? I know, I know eyes, I understand, my *zhena*, my wife, she had accident with eye, I know…"

"Your what?"

She took a step back and blinked at him, tears rolling down her left cheek. One word had got through. "What did you say?"

"I understand the eye, Ganuchka. Let me…"

"No, your something – 'She had accident with eye.'" As she said it, the pain miraculously vanished. The grit had shifted. Furiously she wiped the tears away.

"*Zhena* – my wife. It is nothing."

"Nothing?"

"I see her not. She lives with the small boy, somewhere, I know not. She likes me not."

Wife – small boy – he said it in a flat, careless, throw-away tone. She couldn't believe it. It was a line from a bad play. One hand to her cheek, the other gesturing into the air, she stood helplessly, her brain blown up by a bomb.

He said, "Now is your eye good?"

"Fine. I don't get it – you're *married*?" She could see better now. His face, still misty, kept its creased persuasive smile.

"She from Kharkov. We was been married, but no good. We part – "

"Separated. You've got a *baby*?"

"'Bye, Kostya,' she says. 'We happy with no you. Bye.' No mind this, Ganuchka. Varya and me, we loved a little, so we marry, gain permit for her, gain apartment." Permit! They married just to get a permit! "Then baby, we fight, it over. One and one half years. No more."

"I can't – I don't underst— "

"Ganuchka..." He stepped closer to her. Now he looked tender, confused at her distress. His eyes came towards her, the speckled pupils narrowing as he puzzled it out.

"How could you!" she burst out. "I thought you were..."

I thought you were – what? Young, free, inexperienced like me? Married – divorced! Marriage means mortgages, herbaceous borders, or being a slag who's got herself pregnant and marries any wimp who'll take responsibility... Married – a father? It was bad as finding that – that Dafydd had gone out with Barb Shepherd while she was in Moscow...

New tears blurred his image, and she shouted, "I never want to see you again!" Turning sharply, she ran off in the direction they'd come.

CHAPTER ELEVEN

"But you're going to save him now, aren't you?"

Dostoyevsky, *The Brothers Karamazov*

The suddenness of her movement must have taken him by surprise, because she'd been running for several elongated seconds before she heard "Ganuchka!" behind her, then his footsteps. Her heart moved up into her throat as she ran.

She was wiping tears with one hand, then the other, trying to see where she was going. There were a lot of people on the bridge, and when she bumped into them she gasped, "Sorry!"

She was nearly off the bridge when a huge brown shape loomed towards her. A furry monster growled ferociously, and a mouth full of jagged teeth opened within millimetres of her jeans.

She jerked away – the dog's owner wrenched it back with a barked instruction – and she ran on frantically.

Where was she running to? She must get away from him – be on her own! Curse bloodhounds – curse Russian men!

She saw the steps to the right where they'd come up from the riverside, and dashed down. At the

197

bottom she ran under the bridge, slowed, stopped and leaned against its rough brickwork.

Breathe. Breathe steady. Sniff away tears. She must stop panicking. She was in one piece. Her eye was stinging after the agony of the grit, but it would recover. She could run pretty fast if she put her mind to it. Married – with a baby! That bloody dog! How fast could Kostya run?

She'd nearly stopped crying. She hadn't lost her virginity, or anything else. Only a fraction of heart, plus quite a bit of lust. She'd had a shock, she'd freaked out. But she'd have to talk to him again.

She looked out towards the corner of the bridge. Maybe he'd been scared by the bloodhound – crossed the bridge to avoid it. He'd be here any second.

What would she say to him? "I'm sorry, I panicked, I know I shouldn't mind about you having been married, it's just that it's very unusual in Britain to marry so young..." No – "Just a minute," she'd have to say first, "I'll have to blow my nose."

She reached for her shoulder-bag to get a clean tissue, and her stomach hit her shoes.

Kostya had been carrying her bag. He was an old-fashioned Russian gentleman. He'd got her tissues, her money – not her passport, thank goodness, they'd had to give them to Ellen at the hotel – her hat, her gloves, her precious tiny icon, her map.

Why wasn't he coming? Had he stopped running after her?

He was macho, he'd expect her to come back to

him. He'd be leaning on the decorated iron parapet waiting for her. She'd have to go back and eat humble pie. Then – oh God, it was ten past five already – they'd have to leg it pretty fast to the Arbat!

She pushed herself wearily off the bricks and walked back up the steps to the bridge, composing her words as she went. "Well, who's a stupid twit? 'Twit', there's a new word for your vocabulary." Turning at the top, she visualized his forgiving smile and opened her mouth to apologize.

But he wasn't there. People were walking past her across the bridge, people were over the other side. The bloodhound and its owner had disappeared. So had Kostya.

She walked slowly towards the spot where she'd turned and fled, knowing she'd find him there. She hadn't recognized him immediately because he'd taken his coat off – or he was crouching down, hiding from her, punishing her for her childish fit of temper...

Half-way across, she saw him leaning against the wall at the top of the steps at the far end.

As she got near, he shoved himself off the wall and walked away. It was an older, moustached man in a longer coat. It wasn't him. He wasn't there.

No Kostya. No bag. No money, no map. What had happened to him? How the hell was she going to find her way back?

She turned round. Where in the wilds of Moscow was the Arbat? Miles away! Which side of the Kremlin was it? She'd come into Red Square

near GUM – did she turn up that street there, or
via that garden down by the Kremlin Wall… ?

She looked at her watch. Five-nineteen. She
couldn't possibly get there in time. Would they
wait for her? They'd have to! How would Riina
explain her absence to Ellen and Oleg? Oh God –
Ellen's clipped fury…

Maybe he was down the steps on this side. She
looked back at the bridge. He wasn't coming from
either direction. Yes, she'd try down here. Her
knees trembled as she hurried down.

He wasn't at the bottom of the steps.

She walked back up, exhausted. Don't lose
control. Breathe deeply. Blow your nose on the
scruffy tissue from your pocket.

Her heart and stomach felt weighted down.
What on earth was she going to do? She couldn't
even ask the way! If only she'd learnt a few phrases
of Russian! Could she jump into a taxi and get
Ellen to pay when she got to the Arbat? Nadya and
Riina hadn't been able to get a taxi without hard
currency! She hadn't got a penny or a rouble in her
pocket.

He might have gone to the left off the Kremlin
side of the bridge, away from the onion domes. She
went down and walked on, looking not at where
she was going but at each person she passed. One
of them would be Kostya – one of them must be
Kostya. No. No.

Here were some red coaches parked at a tourist
attraction. What was it? The road looked familiar.

Steam … water … heads bobbing up and down.
It was the open air baths! He wouldn't be here. He

wouldn't be anywhere. Leaden, she retraced her steps. Probably she wouldn't be able to find the bridge again. Then she would be utterly, totally lost.

She would not panic. She – would – not – panic. If she went on walking, thinking, looking around, something would happen to tell her what to do.

Ah. The bridge. At least she'd got some bearings. She climbed up again and saw the red Kremlin Walls. She went back along the pavement by the iron parapet, pausing where she'd turned and run.

She had run ... she had run away before she'd given him Riina's address! There was no more Students' Theatre – if Megan didn't find him, there was no way Riina could see Kostya again!

What, just what, was she going to do? Her knees were jelly-like again, and her feet were sluggish with guilt. They carried her to the far side of the bridge and down the steps.

To her left the river twinkled. The sun was lowering in the sky. The white and gold of the Kremlin was gentle on the far side. There weren't many people here, or traffic. Only mansions of faded elegance set back from the road.

This one here was a mini-palace. Neat, well-painted, in a better state of repair than anywhere else she'd seen in Moscow. Cars were parked on its forecourt, and at the gate stood little sentry boxes with Russian guards in grey coats and fur hats. They were chatting to each other, relaxed.

She stiffened her knees and reached inside her head for some sense. Maybe those sentries could speak a bit of English, might get her a taxi and persuade the driver to take her. She crossed the road.

"Excuse me – " her heart thumped – "do you speak English?"

"Eeengleesh," one said, and they laughed and joked to each other in Russian. Was her face streaked with crying? Her mirror was in her bag!

The other jerked his head towards the gate. "*Passpart?*"

"Pardon?"

"Eeenglish. *Passpart.*" He jerked his head again. "*Britanski.*"

She looked inside the gate, where his gesture indicated. Then she blinked. One of the cars was a Vauxhall, or a Ford. Its number plate was British.

Britanski. Passpart. British. He was asking to see her passport. This was the British Embassy. *Passport problems, visas, personal crises – your piece of British property in the middle of Moscow.*

"I've lost it," she said, trying not to sniff. She hunched her shoulders and splayed her hands in actor's despair. "I have to see the Ambassador."

The face under the fur hat lowered its chin like a reproving teacher. He flung an open hand towards the gate. "Pleess."

"Thank you." She walked through the gate.

Across the forecourt – she felt like stroking the British car – and up the steps under a square pillared canopy. A heavy door, open, with another beyond it. Her legs quivered. What should she do? Ring – knock – wait?

Footsteps behind her. She turned. A broad-faced cheerful man with thick greying hair and a goatee beard was taking the steps two at a time. "Hello there!"

"Er – hello."

"Wanting to come in? Follow me." She followed him.

Inside it was warm. A red carpet stretched out between oak panelled walls. A woman in a floral apron was vacuuming. Wide polished stairs, and portraits of – Gladstone, Wellington? To her left, through an open office door, the Queen and Prince Philip smiled out from a cream wall. On a table lay a tray with an electric kettle, cups and saucers, and a jar of instant coffee. Behind her a man stood on a ladder drilling with a Black and Decker. A *Black* and *Decker*!

"Visa problem or something?" asked the cheerful goatee beard. "We're a bit pressed after the holiday, but if we can help at all…?"

"I'm lost. I've lost everything," she told him, with an air of helpless confidence. "They're waiting for me at the Arbat."

"Ah," he said. "Best hand you over to Her Britannic Majesty's Consul." He reached to a counter behind her and lifted a phone.

Her Britannic Majesty's Consul was tall, dark-suited and clean-shaven, the archetypal stockbroker. He folded his hands and looked at her paternally. She hadn't enough wit left to edit or censor the story, except for the kisses. She told it down to the gift of the precious icon. When she'd finished, he leant back in his upholstered chair, his long fingers tapping its polished wooden arms.

"I see," he said. "Very naughty to abandon your group, you know. Very. What did you say his name was?"

"Kostya."

"Kostya what?"

Had Riina ever told her his surname? "Er – I don't think I ever... Why?"

"It might be known to us, or to the police."

"The *police*?"

"My dear, I'm sorry. He'll have been after your currency."

"No – you misunderstood – it wasn't him who ran away from me, it was me who ran away from — "

"I have to disillusion you. There are a hundred and one techniques. Have you heard about the taxi drivers who pick up Western businessmen from the airport? They 'break down', ask the poor fellow from New York or London to help push, then jump in and drive off. With his currency, portable computers, Lord knows what else in the back."

"But – Kostya..." The man was quite wrong. "Why should he tell me about being married? I don't see how that would — "

"Ask yourself – what made you run off? A neater piece of psychology than most, one must give him credit." He thought Kostya had planned the whole thing from start to finish. "It's quite an aphrodisiac, isn't it? Love across the barricades – the Iron Curtain – the Berlin Wall. Romeo and Juliet weren't the first, and they won't be the last. Heady stuff, Cold War politics." He smiled pleasantly. "Mark my words, young lady. In romance and in politics, the Berlin Wall stands, and it will go on standing."

"You're saying that he — "

"I'm saying that your Romeo is a thief. I've seen it too many times. No tears, please." He folded his hands and leaned forward purposefully. "There are immediate matters to be dealt with. Your group. They're waiting for you."

"At the Arbat." She had to see Riina, and she hadn't told Kostya Riina was wonderful, or given him her address.

"You'll need a car." He turned to a phone and tapped out a few numbers. "John? Have you ten minutes to play chauffeur to a damsel in distress? How long? Good." He put down the phone and stood up. "Would that all my problems were so easily solved, my dear. I recall the Pentre Corach exchange from the correspondence. Miss Tudor-Williams, isn't it? John will deliver you safely into her hands."

"Oh – thanks – you're very…"

"He'll be a few moments. You don't mind waiting in the hall?" He stood up and held out a hand.

It would have seemed a miracle – a car with chauffeur to return her to Ellen and the group. But her head was beating with the Consul's assumptions. He was worse than Ellen! It would make you cynical, dealing with Russian bureaucracy and stolen passports all the time. Something had prevented Kostya following her or waiting for her. Romeo and Juliet – it'd never crossed her mind! She and Kostya found each other attractive. He found her attractive because she came from the West. No! It wasn't true!

She was being whisked through the streets of Moscow like the Queen Mother, and she couldn't care less. All she could think was, Her Britannic Majesty's Consul in Moscow is wrong, and how am I going to face Riina and Ellen.

Kostya would find some way to get in touch! But there was no time, the coach was picking them up before dawn tomorrow morning. Maybe he knew Oleg through the theatre, could contact her via him? But Riina would have known that. No – he was lost. She'd lost him, and lost him for Riina.

She looked at her watch. At this rate she'd be at the Arbat by, what, soon after half past six. More than an hour late! She'd promised Ellen, and broken her promise. Maybe Ellen had thought "Serve her right" and decided to leave without her?

No, she had to deliver each of them home "intact". She could feel the impact of Ellen – Ellen furious, Ellen despairing. "How *could* you, Megan?" But Ellen, you love Oleg, you *know* how I could...

"Oh," she squeaked suddenly. They were approaching the last street before the pedestrianized Arbat. "It was here – the coach was parked here." No coach.

"Well, we'll park here too, then, shall we," said John gruffly, "and we'll see what we shall see." He pulled up beside the pavement, released the seat-belt from round his corpulence and got out.

Pessimism engulfed her as she opened the car door. Kostya had disappeared, so Ellen and the others would have disappeared. Or Riina wouldn't speak to her, or Ellen would kill her with anger.

The cobbled street was crowded. Some artists sat at their easels and a few buskers played in the distance.

A figure ran out from the crowds, followed by another. Ellen! And Riina! She stood, too ashamed to run towards them.

"Well," said John. "Your people, it seems. Miss what-was-it?"

"Tudor-Williams."

"Megan! You are founded!" Riina clasped her. Megan stood stiff.

"Megan! Where on earth – ? We had to let the coach go off... That boy... We were desperate, we thought you'd..."

She gave them a couple of truncated sentences – she'd lost Kostya in the crowds, and with him her shoulder-bag – then introduced John from the Embassy and thanked him as he turned to go. As she heard the car door shut behind her, she realized that one of them was crying, and it wasn't Riina, but Ellen.

Ellen blinked fiercely and said, "House of Culture – we must get back quickly. The parents are there – we're eating at half past seven – I've got to give my speech of thanks..." But she was gasping, and her skin was chalky white.

Riina put a hand on her arm. "House of Culture

must wait. Parents must wait. Five minutes more is no problem. Let us not hurry, let us be slow."

Megan had to apologize. "Ellen, I'm dreadfully sorry. It's your last day, I've ruined it completely – I know, I promised – he wanted to show me all his favourite places in Moscow – like Oleg wanted to show us his favourite church – we had to say goodbye – only we had this row – "

"Thank you, Megan. I accept your explanation. You don't need to elaborate. Can you survive without your bag?"

"I think so – I only had a fiver and a few roubles and a couple of pound coins. I should have kept my eye on the time, I should have thought of you all, of you getting frantic with worry..." How could she say, "Riina, I forgot"?

"No." Ellen was shaking her head. She didn't actually want to know. "Leave it, please. I'm upset about something else. We must go." She turned, and Megan and Riina followed her towards Arbatskaya Station. What did Ellen mean, "something else"? Had something happened to one of the others – to Jim, Abi, Oleg?

She hurried beside Riina. She must explain. Riina would understand that she hadn't had time with Kostya before he told her... Did she know he was married? He'd been secretive with her, Megan, so he was probably secretive with everyone. Secretive, deceitful, calculating. He wanted to go to the West. He wanted her currency – he may have thought her passport was in her shoulder-bag too, he could have used it for forgery...

When they were outside the station, Riina

stopped Ellen. "Please. Is possible to wait moments? I must speak with Megan."

Ellen looked at Megan with a flash of her old impatience. "Come on, Megan. The plot of your personal drama. Please tell us."

"It was true what I said about losing Kostya in the crowds. Only —"

"Only?" Riina's blue eyes turned to Megan. "Is Kostya the bad one? Made he the improper demands, Megan?"

"No, it wasn't that. But the Consul at the Embassy – he said Kostya had it all planned. He was only out for my money."

"Kostya is not that! He is not thief!"

"I know. But he tells lies. Not lies – he hides things."

"What things?" Riina looked ready to defend Kostya on any charge.

"Riina, did you know that Kostya was ... has a wife, he's separated?"

"That youngster?" asked Ellen, harshly. "Well, they all do it, crazy romantic Russians, to get independence and the chance of a flat." Several pieces clicked together in Megan's mind. "Independence" – *Babushka, she died two years ago* – his time with Varya – *one and a half years*. He'd lost his *babushka* at the same time as she needed a residence permit. An impulse marriage, for love – loneliness – convenience.

Riina's head and shoulders were sinking into her coat. "He did not say. I did not know."

"I thought you wouldn't."

"Oh, Riina," Ellen's voice was suddenly soft,

"had you set your heart on this Kostya as well?"

"Riina," Megan burst out, "I'm so sorry. I didn't give him your address. I meant to, but there wasn't time, I got grit behind my contact lens and I was crying and he told me about this wife, and their baby boy – "

"Baby?" Riina turned away. Her shoulders hunched up tight under the long fair hair as if to close the space and stop the words getting through.

Megan touched her arm. "Maybe Oleg can find him. You'd be better for him than me, Riina. You're not stupid and romantic, you care about people…"

She heard something muttered in Russian or Estonian, and then, "Friend. But lover – " she turned on Megan – "lover is what I am wanting being!"

"Don't." Ellen broke in. "If you can be a friend, that's better than anything in the world. Lovers destroy each other." She'd forgotten she was a teacher and was speaking to them wearily, woman to woman. "I'm sorry, Megan. I'll bring you up to date. One or two things happened while we were waiting for you. But – this is for your ears only, OK?"

Megan nodded.

"Oleg and I," she said quietly, "had wondered if … if it was possible to have a relationship. Maybe a permanent one. He might even have come to Clwyd. He very much wants to. But."

"But." Megan could see it. Oleg in North Wales, jobless, penniless, adoring Ellen. Dependent on Ellen, and on the bottle.

"We've talked about their return visit –

Moscow to Pentre Corach. I'd better warn you that it mightn't come off."

"Ellen! Why not? The currency business! Riina, you'll come over anyway?"

"No, it's not the currency. It's that Oleg won't be organizing the second half of the exchange."

"Why not?"

"Because. Because he can't be relied upon."

"But you and he...?"

"I – am fond of him. Very." Ellen turned her head away. "And he of me. This afternoon he swore – he'd never touch another dr— Oh God."

"You wouldn't come here, and live with him in Moscow?"

"Ellen among the vodka bottles? A thousand miles from Wales? Never."

"But she will," Riina said gently to Megan. "She loves him. She will save him."

"I what, Riina?" Ellen leaned forward, alertness fighting the week's exhaustion in her eyes.

"You will come. He needs. You will love and save him."

Ellen shook her head. "It's not possible to save a man, Riina. He's got to do it himself."

"It is possible, Ellen! With a woman's love!"

"No. If... No, it's not possible. I hope that's a lesson you don't have to learn the hard way."

CHAPTER TWELVE

Goodbye old life! Greetings to the new life!

Chekhov, *The Cherry Orchard*

"I've been very naïve," said Ellen as they went down into the station. "Riina's been letting me into a few home truths, Megan. It's not only that Oleg drinks. I knew that well enough. It's that he sells it on the black market."

"We the pupils," said Riina, her voice strong again, "we revere Oleg Stepanovich most greatly. Yet we have had awareness that he has the problem. It is the money which Oleg Stepanovich needs, you understand."

"I suspected all along," said Ellen. "I've been trying to avoid knowing."

"You see, Megan – teachers, most are women in Soviet Union, their salary is not great. A man drinks. Then a man must drink more. So every month he spends every roubles. How does he gain more roubles? He sells the vodka. That is only way for quick money. He tries to fight with his problem – "

"Oh, does he?" Ellen snapped.

"I try to think he does. Levan does not try. He asks Oleg for the vodka."

"At the party..." said Megan. "So they did get it from Oleg."

Ellen put three five-kopek pieces into the machine and they pushed through. "He *trades* in it, Megan. Among young people! A whole network. A teacher, who they should trust! Look how Abi trusts him!"

"Abi? Why Abi?"

Ellen sighed as they walked, but didn't reply till they were on the platform. She offered them each a mint. "You'll have to keep an eye on Abi, Megan. She's developed a crush on Oleg."

"No! I wondered..."

"She burst into tears when we found you'd disappeared, and rushed into his arms for comfort. Annest levered her away and told her to pull herself together – Oleg wasn't worth it – Levan had told her he was dealing in black market drink. Riina thought that if you lot knew, I should know too."

"I am so sorry, Ellen."

"Charisma," Ellen said bitterly. "How *could* I? Abi's one thing, but me! I'm twenty-nine! He filled Gentleman Jim with vodka!"

"No," protested Riina. "Not all blame is to Oleg Stepanovich. Do not hate, Ellen. He is in most respects our dear father. Levan and Vitya, they are big boys, they demand of him the vodka. It is they who fill up Jim. Russian men!"

"They're not all bad – Kostya doesn't drink!" Megan wasn't certain it was true, but she wanted to defend Kostya against something. Though – even if he wasn't an alcoholic or a thief, he was

213

married – a father – he'd abandoned her in the centre of Moscow, maybe because he —

Ellen was looking at Megan with unwavering eyes. She was in control again. "So, you don't believe he's a bad lot?"

"I'm certain he isn't. Riina, you don't think he is, do you?"

Riina suddenly clutched on to Megan, and Megan put her arms round her. "I know not, Megan! I know no thing! I hate Moscow – I will go back to my home in Tallinn and I will study and I will forget all men and all love for ever and ever!"

"Back in Tallinn you'll find the right one, I know you will." She held Riina tight and thought, I'll go home, and I'll study and I'll be back with Dafydd, and I'll have to tell him about Kostya. But how, and what?

A train arrived. Riina pulled away and wiped her eyes. Ellen said, "OK? Ready to get this one?" Riina nodded. They pushed on to the train. There was no hope of a seat. Megan had to fight to stay upright and stop herself knocking against a fat old woman in a grey felt cap reading *Pravda*. She and Riina and Ellen stood close and clutched each other through the worst jerks as the train rattled towards the south west.

"My dear Russian friends," began Ellen, "and Ukrainian and Estonian and Georgian friends. This has been one of the most significant weeks of my life."

Round the table with its empty champagne bottles and plates with the remains of caviar and *shashlik*, faces were all turned towards Ellen. Even the mothers, who had shopped for and cooked and served the meal, sat down at a side table.

Oleg had kept a place for Ellen beside him, and Riina found an empty seat between Annest and Meredydd. Megan saw a seat two places away from Abi, and got Tie and Mike to budge up so that she could sit next to her.

Everyone absorbed her back into the scene without question. In the five-thirty crisis Riina had told them they'd got separated in a crowd. Mish just came and put an arm briefly on her shoulder as if to say "Thank God you've arrived". There was an empty seat between Mrs Haigh and Mrs Garth Jones: Sylvia the guide was at the Salyut Hotel waiting for confirmation of their return flight, and Mr Haigh had been deputed to check that everything was fixed.

"It has been," said Ellen, "a week full of what we in Wales call *hwyl* – liveliness, gusto. Now we feel that other sensation the Welsh express so well – *hiraeth*, a longing for home. We've learnt many things this week. One thing we've learnt is that every person feels *hiraeth* for their own place. Though each person can love another country, nowhere will ever be the same as their own home."

Then she began the thank-yous. She thanked the parents in turn, and the young people for their friendliness and enthusiasm during this wonderful trip. She even remembered to thank the officials, including those at the British Embassy in Moscow, for their help in administration.

She'd just got as far as thanking Nina's mother

and Mrs Haigh for their contribution to first aid when Megan's brain lurched into Kostya gear again. What about her bag? She didn't believe... He'd bring it back somehow. He'd find Oleg's address in the phone directory... No phone directory.

There was always the Salyut Hotel. Hotel – kiss in lift – ticket for bedroom – how could she have got so carried away with romance? – Romeo and Juliet, the Berlin Wall, *There's a place for us...* "Oh!" In a flash she realized that something else was in her bag, in Kostya's possession. The container for her contact lenses! They had to be kept in special fluid overnight – they were ruined if you put them down on a surface or wrapped them in a hankie...

But she held her lips tight shut. Kostya or no Kostya, bag or no bag, she wasn't going to cause any more commotion.

"...And lastly, of course, to Oleg, without whom – " Ellen's voice came over strong and controlled – "none of this would have been possible. None of his efforts, none of his kindnesses, will ever be forgotten.

"I think back," she went on, her voice slipping in volume, "to when I visited Moscow last, in March. It was the beginning of spring, the time when the ice on the Moskva River, which has been locked solid for months, starts to melt. Ice, melting. That's the picture that will come up in my mind when I think of Moscow – of the Soviet Union. When ice melts, the water starts to run free. But ice-floes, icebergs, break away into the running water. And those great boulders of ice collide. They crash into each other. You can't have change without pain.

"But – " she went on, after a sharp intake of breath – "we from the Pentre Corach Drama Club have been privileged to take part in the melting process. No one knows what will happen next, in politics or in our friendships. All we can be sure of, is that this has been a week none of us will ever forget." She sat down amid applause.

Oleg stood up. What would he say? With his ill-fitting suit he wore a flamboyant yellow spotted tie that must surely be a present from the West. Had he been drinking? There wasn't a champagne bottle within reach. Had Ellen made sure of that, or was he still hoping to persuade her? Had she told him that their relationship was finally off, and she wouldn't let him organize a return trip? Would someone else lead it? It was impossible – the group would fold without him.

"My dear Pentre Corach – my dear Yelyena," he began. Ellen had her head bowed. "How can I say what is in my heart? I composed a speech – " he took a sheaf of ragged pages from his breast pocket – "but it will not suffice. What will suffice for this moment?"

He's going to have us all wiping our eyes on the tablecloths, thought Megan. She looked at Abi. Can she survive this? What will she be like on the plane on the way home? I'll stick by her. I'll go around with Mish sometimes, but I won't drop Abi. I'd no idea she'd got it in her to fall for someone like Oleg.

Abi was staring at Oleg, her eyes open very wide. Her left hand was on her knee with a screwed up hankie clutched in it. On her far side sat Nina, and beyond Nina, Jim.

There were some sounds from behind which Megan ignored. She thought it was the odd mother still bustling about.

"The future is a mountain, covered by misty fog," Oleg declared. "Currency – many other problems – make it difficult for us to see the path ahead. The path also is not clear towards our return visit to you, dear friends. But maybe, maybe – things happen, unheard of things. West may meet East, East may meet West... It appears, my friends, that East German governments may change. Even tonight, I hear that the whole, the entire Politburo in East Berlin has resigned.

"After that, who knows?" He cleared his throat. "And for us – who knows? It is possible that — "

Someone was tapping Megan on the shoulder. She looked up, expecting to be offered some tea or coffee. It was Mr Haigh, bending low.

"Um – Megan – I have something for you," he whispered, his eyebrows high up into his forehead with embarrassment. "Perhaps you would..." He moved back towards the door, clutching something to his front.

Megan, not looking at Riina or Abi or anyone, slipped out of her chair as unobtrusively as she could. She tiptoed over to where Mr Haigh was standing in the doorway.

He held out her shoulder-bag.

"A young man came to the hotel. He approached our guide with this. I was not there at the time, I had to go... Hum. Our guide looked inside. The bag appeared to have your name in it. You mislaid it, perhaps?" Megan took the bag. She felt it might fall to pieces or vanish from her hand.

"I thought it best to deliver it at the earliest possible opportunity, since our flights are now satisfactorily confirmed... I trust nothing has gone astray."

"Thank you. Thanks very much, Mr Haigh, it's very kind... I'll just go outside for a moment and check everything's still there."

She moved out into the corridor. Mr Haigh strode over to join the banquet.

Shaking, she unclipped the buckle of her bag and lifted the flap.

Gloves. Yellow hat. Tissues. Chocolate. Comb. Inhaler. Diary. Map of Moscow. Contact lens bottle. The usual few odd scraps of paper. Purse.

Feeling faithless, she took out the purse and opened it. In the wallet section, a five-pound note and various roubles. In the purse, three pound coins and some kopeks. Kostya was not a thief. Kostya – was – not – a – thief.

She let out an "Oh!" of relief and remorse. Of *course* he – how *could* she... That wretched Britannic Consul! Kostya – he was true, sad, loving, angry... But why hadn't he come after her? Was he attacked by that dog? Or did he mean to steal her currency, then have a fit of conscience later? No! He loved her – he gave her the...

The icon. Where was it? She shoved the purse

under her arm and scrabbled through her bag again. Hat – diary – map… No icon. He'd taken it back.

One of the scraps of paper wasn't folded, and it had large, childlike writing on it that she didn't recognize. She snatched it out.

All it said was, *You were not trusting me, Ganuchka.*

No, she hadn't trusted him. *You were not trusting.* She could have trusted him.

She heard some sort of uproar at the banquet through the door. What was going on? She wanted to see Riina and tell her – show her the bag, the note. She stuffed everything back into the bag.

When she got through the door, she couldn't think how Oleg's speech could have ended to produce what she saw. All the Moscow teenagers were on their feet. They were shouting something like "No, my apartment is"; "No, mine, mine". Ellen and Oleg were trying to calm them down and get some sort of order out of the chaos.

Mish spotted Megan and came over. "What's up? I thought you'd gone off again!"

"No, I'd lost my bag – Mr Haigh found it…"

"Meggo, you look whacked out. I did wonder… Look, tell me tomorrow. Abi's dad says —"

"What on earth's going on?"

"Abi's dad came with the news that something's happening – we don't know what – at the Berlin Wall. Everyone wants to get near a TV, and they're arguing about whose flat's the nearest."

"Well, I'd say Riina's is," said Megan.

Calm was settling at the tables, and as Megan and Mish went to take their places Oleg announced, "It seems sure that Riina Tormis has the closest home. Transport – it is some twenty minutes to walk, I think – but I believe some parents have cars parked nearby? May I ask? One – two – three... Thank you."

"Come!" commanded Riina. Playing her part as hostess, she took Ellen's arm, and Megan found herself taking Oleg's, and in a few minutes they were all squashed in Masha's father's big black car with Masha and Mish and Nadya on their way to the Tormises' flat.

The moment they got through the door, Riina ran to the kitchen and switched on the radio. Then she ran to the living room and turned on the TV. Hardly anyone stayed in the kitchen. Most of them hurried to the living room to sit or stand or perch with their eyes glued to the box in the corner. When the other car-loads arrived, they packed themselves down on the floor or leaned against the walls.

Megan went into the living room and squeezed on to the sofa with Abi and Nadya and Mish. She gazed at the unintelligible TV, her head still bursting with Kostya. Had he perhaps taken her address from her diary – might he write to her? If he did, she could tell him to contact Riina, she could give him her address. She passionately, overwhelmingly wanted him to write, to say he loved her and had run after her, it was just that the bloodhound...

But just as passionately she wanted him not to. Home was home, her own territory, Dafydd's territory. How could she tell Dafydd everything? How could she *not* tell Dafydd everything? Oh – home! She was worn to a frazzle. Please, let's get home soon. Let this evening end, let Berlin do whatever Berlin's going to do and let's just get *home*.

More were arriving – the parents who had walked. Mr and Mrs Tormis had given up trying to say "Welcome" to everyone. Where was Riina?

The living room was getting impossibly full. In one corner Jim and Nina stood close, their arms round each other, their eyes straying from the television back to each other's faces every five seconds. Annest was sitting in a chair with Levan at her feet, her hand hanging down and linked with his. Olwen was squashed in a chair with Masha, Dima and Vitya perching on the arms.

"Maybe," said Olwen, "maybe Soviet tanks are rolling into East Germany now, like they rolled into Czechoslovakia in 1968 and Hungary in '56..." Ellen and Oleg were standing on either side of the door, their eyes turned firmly away from each other, towards the TV.

Riina didn't seem to be anywhere. She must be in the kitchen, Megan thought. I must tell her I've got my bag back, and show her Kostya's note. "Back in a minute," she murmured to Mish, easing herself up.

"No running off," said Mish.

"Who, me?" Megan gave her a small kick and pushed her way to the door.

At the door, Ellen caught her arm. "Megan?"

Megan showed Ellen her bag. "He took it to the hotel. I'm going to show Riina."

"I noticed, in the car. He was a good one, then? But why didn't he run after you?"

"There was this dog... I don't know. Is Riina in the kitchen?"

"I think so." Ellen let her go. The front door was open again and more parents were squeezing in.

Megan manoeuvred her way through the hall. In the kitchen, she shoved round the Welskis chatting with Mike and Seriozha who were perched on top of the table. Riina was squashed beside the window-sill, her ear as close as possible to the radio. She looked up as Megan came near.

"Riina, look." Megan fumbled in her bag and took out Kostya's note. "He came to the hotel. He took back the present he'd given me, and left me this." As she said it, tears began to come. In a blur, she handed over the scribbled page.

"Megan!" Riina looked up from the note, then read it again. "'*You were not...*' Oh, Megan! '*Trusting me*'!"

"Sssssh!" Seriozha hissed suddenly from behind them. "*Vremya!*"

The radio was giving its electronic snatch of *Moscow Nights*.

"Ssssssh!" said Riina, and Megan took it up. "Ssshh! News!" Everyone went quiet.

Again, Megan wished she spoke Russian. She gazed at the radio, willing it to say a word she could understand. What was the man saying?

Riina's eyes were wide. Behind her, Mike and Seriozha gasped.

"It is!" breathed Riina. "It is! Open! The Wall! They have opened it – the Berlin Wall! People are coming through from East to West – West to East, even!"

"They've opened the Wall!" Megan could hardly take in what it meant. *The Berlin Wall stands, and will go on standing*. But it wouldn't. It was open, and it would come down.

Riina dropped Kostya's note on to the kitchen floor, and Megan dropped her shoulder-bag. Sniffing away tears, they flung their arms round each other, and the news flew round the room and out of the door.

And so I went out into the world.

Gorky, *My Childhood*

Megan and Dafydd sat cuddled together on the sofa watching television. Mum and Dad, like half the rest of the world, were in bed with flu, and Kate had been banished to Jason's for Christmas to keep her away from infection – which was good because it meant the ultimate stamp of Dad's approval for Jason, but bad because Jason's parents turned out to be deadly strict about leaving the two of them alone together.

Dad and Mum, languishing upstairs, had no interest in what Megan and Dafydd were doing. Mum spent most of the time fast asleep in one room, while Dad filled the other room with moans about his aching limbs and the mindless rubbish on all TV channels over Christmas. Every so often Megan would take up cups of tea to wash down their aspirins and vitamins, and offer hot water bottles or cooling flannels depending on the state of the thermometer.

"All right?" asked Dafydd as Megan came down for the fourth time.

225

"Dad's thrown a slipper at Cilla Black," said Megan, stroking the cat on Dafydd's knee. She knelt beside the fire and rearranged the logs with the poker.

"Sign of energy, eh?"

Megan's face was hot from the fire. She was about to turn round when a spark flew up, glowing against the blackened stones of the chimney. Sparks against the blackness – against the black sky of Moscow – Kostya's warmth against her back... Kostya. Memories exploded – lustful memories, painful memories, confused memories – the moon over the University, the bedroom ticket, his face glowing in candlelight in front of the icon, the grit on the bridge...

"Megan? *Gâd i ni fynd am dro.*"

She blinked and put the poker back on its stand. Her Welsh was coming on, but it needed all her concentration. "Er – OK. It isn't raining, is it? Let's go down the lane. But back in time for the news."

She shouted up to her parents and she and Dafydd went out. It was mild and cloudy with no moon to see by, so they'd brought a torch. Megan shone it down the lane and beamed it on mossy walls and tree trunks. Everything was inhabited by friendly ghosts. She'd fallen in love with the Clwyd landscape since coming back from Moscow. "The hills – trees – all the little walls and lanes, the nooks and crannies..." Dafydd couldn't imagine the flatness of Moscow, the endless bleak space, even when she showed him the photos.

They'd had Christmas dinner with the Morgans. Dafydd's grandparents always gave

Megan a big welcome, though his mother was shy, knowing that the Shipways had seen her during her bad times. They were pleased as punch about Megan learning Welsh, though they couldn't understand how she'd been persuaded to it by her Estonian friend in Moscow.

"It'll be Riina's last Christmas in Moscow," she said to Dafydd. She felt his hand in hers. A tentative hand, compared with Kostya's. It was comfortable, she could relax with it. But why hadn't she told him about Kostya? Didn't she trust him to understand? No, she'd felt too raw. "You were not trusting me." OK, she could have trusted him not to steal her money. But he gave nothing of himself. He wouldn't let her know him.

She knew that the pain showed. She'd blushed in front of the family, several times, when things Russian had come up – trivial things, about *babushkas*, the smallness of flats, the shortage of soap. When letters came from Riina, her heart went like the clappers and she grabbed the letter and rushed upstairs. Her parents asked no questions – they seemed to recognize Moscow as a turning point in Megan's life. But how could she risk blushes and heart-poundings with Dafydd?

"D'you think she'll ever get over here to see you?" asked Dafydd.

"I suppose it'll depend on what happens to Estonia – whether they get their freedom." Riina hadn't bumped into Kostya, neither had she tried to find him. "Nadya has encountered Yuri," she wrote. "She says to me that he will entice Kostya towards me if I request it. But I tell her no. Since your departure, Megan, all my mind has been on our return to Tallinn in March." Of course, no letter from Kostya had arrived in Clwyd. Megan was glad.

Dafydd didn't tease her about watching the TV news and reading the paper, but she knew he found it puzzling. Abi was taking an interest too, partly because Jim was collecting newspaper clippings about all things Soviet. Jim was corresponding with Nina – it was still true love between them – but in the meanwhile, Abi and Jim were very good friends. Mr and Mrs Haigh now thought Jim "a splendid young man".

Dafydd had been up at the Shipways' three days ago when Megan was glued to every TV news bulletin about Romania – Ceausescu's fall, escape and capture. "A helicopter has lifted him from the top of the building... He has commandeered a private car... Mr and Mrs Ceausescu are escaping in a red car..." Even Kate and Jason got caught up in the on-going drama of the world's most hated tyrant.

At school Megan found she wasn't alone in being stunned by the news from Eastern Europe. First, East Germany and the Berlin Wall. Then Czechoslovakia's Velvet Revolution. And now Romania toppling Ceausescu. Megan found it hard to absorb the news at that pace. She and Mish and Olwen met in town and talked about it over a Coke.

"Nadya says it was us that did it!" Mish rustled pages of scrawly letter. "'You came – the Berlin Wall was made open – and now, look!' She seems to have chucked poor Yuri – she's on about someone called Andrei." They speculated about what might happen between Ellen and Oleg when they met, as promised, at the remains of the Berlin Wall on 9th November 1990. It was anyone's guess.

Dafydd and Megan only did a small circuit round the lanes, so as to be back to tend Mum and Dad and in time for the news. They walked past the lighted windows of the stone cottages in the village. Megan knew who lived in each cottage, except the new family who'd bought the Evans' after the last of the three ancient sisters had faded away and died. If things had been different, she might have lived in a tiny flat high up in a vast impersonal block in a Milky Way of identical blocks in Moscow. Or Tallinn, Estonia. Or Bucharest, Romania. In which case...

"Come on home, Megan *bach*." Dafydd squeezed her hand.

"Sorry, Daf."

Back home, Megan took off her coat and ran up the stairs two at a time. She found Mum and Dad snoozing in their separate rooms, Dad clutching his other slipper to throw at the celebrity who next offended him. The commercials were just finishing.

Dafydd had taken off his shoes, and his long legs stretched out from the sofa towards the fire. I can imagine it, thought Megan – him, me, the cottage, the cat, the fire. But there's more to life than that. There's the rest of the world – I want that too. Does he?

She switched the TV on and stretched out beside him. He twined his arm round hers automatically. The news was just beginning.

I know what the difference is, thought Megan, between the news then, before Moscow, and the news now, after. It's that I know it's truly happening. It's happening to real live people. It could be happening to me. I never believed it before. I can't say that to Dafydd – it sounds too pretentious.

The concerned face made its formal announcement. "The headlines tonight. President Ceausescu of Romania and his wife have been shot."

Dafydd sat bolt upright. "Shot!" He flopped back and they watched the rest of the bulletin in silence.

When it was over Megan switched off, then stood looking at Dafydd. "It gets to you, doesn't it?"

He nodded. "They hated him, that man, didn't they."

"Daf – you know Spock's going to the Tech... Will you come and play keyboard on the next Moscow trip?"

Dafydd looked surprised. "I've never thought... All right, if Ellen'll have me. I might do that."

"It's just..." Megan bounced down on to the sofa again. "I'm caught up in it now. It seems that it's all about me, as well as about them."

"Well, it's about Riina and Nina and Nadya and all, isn't it? They're your friends."

"Yes." She settled herself beside him and said, "And Kostya – did I tell you about Kostya?"

"No?" said Dafydd. "Which one's she?"